**"I've brought someone with me,"
Rafael told her, as he lifted
something up and deposited it
on the bed.**

Totally bemused, Serena realized that
she was staring at a carrycot, and inside,
dressed in soft blue cotton, tiny feet bare,
lay a small baby.

"Oh! He's *gorgeous!*" she exclaimed. "What's
his name?"

"I call him Tonio."

"He's yours? I didn't know you were
married."

"I'm not."

"Then Tonio.... He's a—a—love-child?"

"A love-child?" Rafael's mouth twisted
cynically on the word. "There are those
who would call him something far less
complimentary."

"But if you and his mother are together...."

"No!" It came out forcefully. "Tonio's mother
and I are *not* together."

He's a man of cool sophistication.
He's got pride, power and wealth.
At the top of his corporate ladder,
he's a ruthless businessman—an *expert* lover
His life runs like a well-oiled machine....

Until now.
Because suddenly he's responsible for a BABY!

His Baby
A miniseries from Harlequin Presents®.
He's sexy, successful...
and he's facing up to fatherhood!

There'll be another HIS BABY title out soon.

Kate Walker

RAFAEL'S LOVE-CHILD

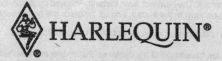

HARLEQUIN®

TORONTO • NEW YORK • LONDON
AMSTERDAM • PARIS • SYDNEY • HAMBURG
STOCKHOLM • ATHENS • TOKYO • MILAN • MADRID
PRAGUE • WARSAW • BUDAPEST • AUCKLAND

For Doctor Cathy
With thanks for all the information and advice

ISBN 0-373-12160-1

RAFAEL'S LOVE-CHILD

First North American Publication 2001.

Copyright © 2000 by Kate Walker.

CHAPTER ONE

'DO YOU know who you are?'

The question came sharply, making Serena blink in confusion as she struggled to focus on her surroundings. Her mind seemed clogged and hazy, her thoughts strangely fuzzy round the edges.

'What a silly question—of course I know who I am! My name is Serena Martin. And...'

Frowning slightly, brown eyes narrowed in concentration, she ran a disturbed hand through the bright auburn of her hair as she looked round her, taking in the pastel-toned room, the soft peach and cream curtains that matched the cover on the bed in which she lay. In spite of obvious attempts to make it look attractive, the bedroom still had an impersonal, institutional feel. And the dark-haired woman who sat beside her bed, her grey eyes fixed on Serena's face, wore a tailored white coat that told its own story.

'...and I presume this is a hospital of some kind?'

'That's right.'

'And do you know what happened?'

Two voices sounded this time, chiming together so that it was almost impossible to tell them apart. But it was enough to make Serena realise that that the woman in the white coat—the doctor—was the one who had reassured her, not the one asking all the questions.

They were coming from the man on the opposite side of the room. The man whose powerful frame filled the doorway in which he stood, strong back ramrod-straight, broad shoulders squared.

He was tall, dark, definitely imposing—frighteningly so.

Frighteningly? The word brought Serena up sharp. She

5

was sure she had never seen this man in her life before, so where had that description come from? She couldn't say, only knew that it seemed disturbingly appropriate.

'Do you?' he insisted now, the intriguing accent that she had caught so briefly a moment before deepening with the emphasis of his tone. 'Can you tell me how you came to be here?'

That was much more difficult. If she hunted in her mind for the answer to his question, all she found was confusion, tangled, clouded thoughts and vague memories. There were muddled impressions of noise and panic, a sickening crash and someone screaming in fear.

Was that someone herself?

'I—I presume there must have been some sort of accident.'

'What kind of accident?'

For all that he hadn't moved from his position at the door, the way that the man spoke made Serena feel as if he had actually stepped further into the room, coming dangerously close to her and seeming to pin her against the wall.

'I—I don't know!' For the first time she faced him head-on, turning defiant brown eyes on his dark face. 'Why don't *you* tell me?'

Who was he? Another doctor? He wasn't wearing the regulation white coat that revealed the occupation of the woman who still sat at her bedside. Instead, his lean frame was encased in the sort of dark suit whose exquisite fabric and perfect tailoring screamed the sort of perfection only a great deal of money could buy.

But perhaps he was of some higher rank than the friendly woman—a surgeon, or a consultant. Wasn't it the case that they didn't wear white coats, just as they were addressed as 'Mr' and not 'Doctor'?

Whoever he was, he was stunning, impossibly handsome. Looking at him was like looking into the brightness of the sun, the effect on every one of her senses was so devastating.

That impressive height was combined with jet-black hair,

sleek and heavy, brushed back from his face in a way that emphasised his superbly carved cheekbones. Dazedly Serena became aware of a straight, jutting nose, determined chin and surprisingly sensual mouth, but it was the eyes that she noticed most. Fringed by impossibly thick, luxuriantly black lashes, they were deep gold, almost the colour of flame and blazing just as brightly.

And the rich tan that bronzed this man's skin was not the result of some two-week Mediterranean holiday. Instead it was obviously his natural colouring, the year-round tone that came from an ancestry that was definitely not English.

Unconsciously, Serena shifted slightly in the bed, feeling suddenly too warm, too restless to stay still. There was a new, pagan wildness in her blood, one that drove her heart faster, pushing hot colour into her cheeks, making her sharply aware of the fact that under the bedclothes she was only wearing a short, regulation hospital nightdress.

And the truly disturbing thing was that she could see her own feelings reflected in this man's eyes, in the black, enlarged pupils, the intensity of his gaze, even though his expression never altered but stayed as coolly assessing as before. The contrast between that apparently calm control and the blaze of something very different and very primitive in his gaze dried her mouth and throat so that she had to swallow hard to relieve them.

'What makes you think I can tell you anything?' he flung at her now, his accent deepening on the words in a way that confirmed her suspicions about his ancestry.

'Mr Cordoba...' the doctor put in quietly, warningly, but both Serena and her inquisitor ignored the interjection, their attention focused solely on each other.

'Well, I presume I'm supposed to know you.'

'Not at all!'

An arrogant little flick of his long-fingered hand dismissed her comment as nonsense.

'On the contrary, you have never seen me before in your life.'

Well, that was a relief. She was sure that if she had come up against this man at any time in her past she would remember him—with bells on! She didn't know how she had come to be here, in this hospital, had no idea what had happened to her, but she definitely felt easier knowing that this—what had the doctor called him?— this Mr Cordoba had played no part in her life before.

'Then who *are* you?'

'My name is Rafael Cordoba.'

Clearly he expected that that would mean something to her. Serena could only wish that it did. Right now she would be grateful for anything that would explain this Rafael Cordoba's presence in her room. Anything to get him off her back, stop this unnerving string of questions.

No, if she was honest, what she really wanted was to be free of this restless, unsettled feeling that he created in her. Never before had she felt so intensely physically aware of anyone, and the decidedly carnal nature of the thoughts he sparked off in her brain was making it so very difficult to concentrate on anything else.

'And you...?' Serena turned to the woman at her bedside, a friendly, sympathetic face in the middle of this confusion and uncertainty.

'I'm Dr Greene.' To her relief the other woman stepped into the breach, answering the mute appeal of her patient's deep brown eyes. 'Do you feel up to answering some questions?'

'I'll try.'

It was a struggle to ignore Cordoba. Even though she forced herself to concentrate on the doctor, she could still see him out of the corner of her eye. His presence in the doorway was like a bruise at the back of her mind, dark and ominous.

'Your name is Serena Martin?'

'That's right.'

'And you are how old?'

'Twenty-three.'

Slowly Serena started to relax. This was easier. Dr Greene's quiet questions posed no problems, carried no threats. And the confusion in her thoughts that had so disturbed her at first was gradually starting to clear. She couldn't have suffered any real ill-effects if her answers came as quickly and easily as this.

'Can you tell me your address?'

'Thirty-five Alban Road, Ryeton... What is it?' Serena questioned sharply as the pen which had been writing busily suddenly stopped and the doctor turned surprised eyes on her face.

'Ryeton in Yorkshire?'

'Yes.'

'Then what are you doing in London?'

It was that voice again. The one with the accent that lifted all the little hairs at the back of her neck, sent shivers skittering down her spine. She should have known that Cordoba couldn't bring himself to stay quiet for long.

'L-London? I—is that where we are?'

'Where this hospital is,' he put in curtly, ignoring the reproving glance Dr Greene turned in his direction. 'Where you are, where the accident took place, where—'

'That's enough, Mr Cordoba!'

But Rafael Cordoba was clearly not at all concerned by the doctor's intervention, his dark head coming up arrogantly, golden eyes flashing rejection of her reproof as he took a couple of swift, forceful strides into the room.

'So what were you doing here, if you live in—?'

'I don't know!' Serena had reached the end of her tether. Her head was aching and she felt exhausted, wrung out, as if she had just run a marathon. Frantically she shook her head, tears of weakness filling her eyes, blurring the sight of his darkly intent face. 'Perhaps I'm on holiday. Perhaps...'

'I said *enough*!' Dr Greene was clearly not in any way

over-awed or cowed. But then she continued on a softer, more conciliatory note, one that revealed she was far from under-impressed by this man's forceful presence, 'I have my patient to think of. Miss Martin is easily tired. She has been through something of an ordeal, the sort of thing that would set anyone back, let alone someone who was already rather rundown. She needs rest, and I must insist that she gets it.'

And that was obviously not what he wanted to hear, Serena thought hazily as she saw the flare of anger in those amazing eyes, the temper that fought against the strict control he imposed on it so that the beautiful mouth clamped into an uncompromisingly hard line.

In that moment it was as if she had known him for ever, so recognisable were the danger signs in his face. Whoever he was, he certainly wasn't accustomed to being opposed by someone he obviously considered his inferior. His breath hissed in through his teeth as he prepared to speak.

But then, just as she had nerved herself for the explosion that she felt sure was about to break over the doctor's unsuspecting head, he clearly reconsidered his position. That forceful jaw snapped shut on the angry words he had been about to utter, closing with such force that Serena actually heard the click of his teeth as they came together.

'As you wish!' he declared icily.

Satisfied that he was going to keep silent, at least for the moment, Dr Greene turned back to Serena.

'Is there anyone we can contact for you? Your parents? Some other next of kin?'

'No.' Despondently she shook her head. 'My parents are no longer alive. My mother died of cancer last year and my father had a fatal heart attack eighteen months before that. There's no one.'

Once more she had to struggle against the sting of tears, blinking furiously to hold them back as the doctor leaned forward and placed a reassuring hand on hers.

'You really must not get upset. You need to rest and take things quietly, recuperate...'

'But how can I rest until I know what happened?' Serena's voice quavered weakly on the words. How could anyone expect her to relax until she had been told exactly how she had come to be here, in this hospital, and just what had happened before that?

Because she could remember nothing of what must have been an accident that had so knocked her for six that she hadn't even been aware of having been brought to the hospital and put in this bed. And if she was in London...

'Please!' Reaching out, she caught hold of the doctor's hand, clinging onto it as if it was her only lifeline, the one weak link with sanity in a world that suddenly seemed to have gone completely mad. 'You must tell me! How did I come to be here?'

'You had an accident.' Dr Greene spoke with obvious reluctance. 'You were in a car crash and you had a rather nasty bang on the head. You've been completely out of it for a while.'

'A while? How long is a while?'

'It's almost ten days now. You were deeply unconscious at first, but just lately you've been drifting in and out.'

'I have?'

Frowning hard, Serena forced herself to concentrate. If she really tried, it was just possible to recall vague moments that she had thought she had dreamed. Moments of seeming to struggle to the surface of some clouded, murky pond, reaching frantically for footholds or something to cling on to.

Then, just for a few tiny, brief seconds, she had been able to open her eyes and look around, barely managing to focus before the heavy, sticky darkness had descended once more and folded around her, cutting her off again.

'There was someone...'

Someone had been sitting by the bed, watching and waiting for her to wake. Someone who had heard the unhappy, troubled sounds she had made as she stirred restively, struggling against the nightmares that enclosed her. Someone who had smoothed the tangled copper hair back from her hot forehead with a cool, soothing hand.

And, later, someone who had poured her water and held her as she struggled to drink, gently dissuading her from gulping as she strained to ease her parched and aching throat.

'Someone was here...'

'A nurse. You've been under strict observation.'

'No...'

It hadn't been a nurse. She had no idea how she knew that, but it was the one point on which she was absolutely positive. The good Samaritan, the soft voiced helper who had tended to her in the darkness of the night, at her lowest moments, had not had the coolly professional approach, the detached, impersonal restraint of a trained carer. And the voice she had heard...

The *voice*!

Wide and rounded with shock, her brown eyes flew to Rafael Cordoba's face, clashing harshly with the stony golden gaze he turned on her. The beautifully carved features could have been sculpted from bronze marble, showing no response at all as he deliberately blanked out her questioning glance, stonewalling, giving away nothing at all.

'You have had the best care that money could buy, Miss Martin,' he said coolly, as if that was the unspoken question she had asked him.

But she didn't really need to ask anything. She knew what she had heard, and she had heard that accent soothing her, comforting her in the darkness of the night. So why had he now turned from ministering angel into Spanish Inquisitor?

'But...' she began, then wearily shook her aching head. 'I need to know...'

Her voice seemed beyond her control, fading weakly into a sigh she could not suppress.

'You're tired,' Dr Greene put in gently. 'You must be careful not to overdo things at this early stage. You know as much as you can cope with right now. You need to rest.'

Wearily Serena nodded. She *was* tired. Her thoughts were sliding out of focus, that fuddled, heavy feeling like cotton wool back inside her head. Lacking the strength to stay upright, she sank back against her pillows, heavy eyelids drooping.

'I'll be back to talk to you again soon. Everything will be all right.'

'Everything!' It was a harsh exclamation, slashing into the silence that had descended as Rafael moved suddenly, one hand coming up in a violent gesture. 'Everything! *Madre de Dios*, what about—?'

'Mr Cordoba!' There was real annoyance in the doctor's voice now. 'I said *enough*! I want you to go now—to leave Miss Martin alone.'

He was tempted to rebel against her instructions, it was obvious. Once more that dangerous anger flared in his eyes, in the darkly searing glance he flung at the doctor and then, unnervingly, at Serena herself. But a couple of seconds later he drew himself up again, that strong jaw setting determinedly.

'Very well,' he said, each word cold and clipped and icily precise, heightening his accent strongly. 'I'll go. But...'

The turn of his head, the direction of his eyes, made it plain that the next thing he said was for Serena alone.

'I'll be back,' he said, low and hard, and deadly. 'I promise you that. I'll be back just as soon as I can.'

They were only words, Serena tried to tell herself as she shrank back in the bed, pulling the covers up close around her. Only words. Almost the same ones that the doctor had used just a few moments before.

But she had seen Rafael Cordoba's eyes as he spoke, seen the dangerous gleam in them, the burn of something that made her shiver inwardly, and as a result his promise to re-

turn had had precisely the opposite effect to the reassurance
that Dr Greene had given her.

He would be back; she could have no doubt about that.
And the honest truth was that the prospect of coming face to
face with him again was one that made her shudder in fearful
apprehension.

CHAPTER TWO

'I'VE brought someone to see you.'

'What?'

Serena glanced up from the magazine she had been staring at listlessly, not taking in a single word, her eyes going to where the man who had spoken stood in the doorway.

Rafael Cordoba, of course. Who else would it be?

It was five days now since the disturbing, confusing moment when she had woken from unconsciousness to find herself here in this hospital and on the receiving end of Rafael's forceful questioning. 'I'll be back,' he had promised, and he had kept firmly to that promise. The very next morning he had appeared at her bedside, and every day since.

But it was obvious that Dr Greene or someone in a position of even higher authority had had a word or two with him before he had been let into the ward. The hard, aggressive tone had been muted, the curt, sharp questions silenced, temporarily at least, and even the powerful sexual awareness she had sensed in him had been ruthlessly reined in.

'I'm sorry—what did you say?'

She prayed that he would take the unevenness in her voice, the faint quaver she couldn't quite suppress, as the result of being taken by surprise by his unexpected arrival. The last thing she wanted him to suspect was the sheer, mind-blowing, physical effect he had on her simply by existing. Just the sight of that long, lean body, the jet-black hair and burning golden eyes made her breath catch in her throat, her heart stumbling in its natural rhythm.

And today it was even worse. On every other occasion on which she had seen him, he had been dressed in an immaculately cut suit like the one he had been wearing on that first day. But today, perhaps as a concession to the heat of the sun outside, he had thrown off that formality, opting instead for casual jeans and a short-sleeved shirt.

The tight denim hugged the firm lines of his narrow waist and hips, emphasising his masculinity in a way that was sinfully sensual, and the pure white cotton of his shirt contrasted starkly with the bronzed skin at his arms and throat, making it seem darker and warmer as a result.

Nervously Serena twitched at the peach-coloured cover on her bed, painfully aware of the amount of pale, lightly freckled skin exposed by the sleeveless vee-necked top of her cream cotton nightdress. She longed to cover up, but feared that any unwise movement would simply draw his attention to the way she was feeling.

'I've brought someone with me...'

'Another visitor? That's a surprise. I didn't think I knew anyone in London.'

Her memory of the accident, and the days leading up to it, had still not returned, and in a way that she found intensely frustrating neither the doctor nor Rafael was prepared to give her any information on the subject.

'You have to be patient,' was the response she heard every time she asked a question or fretted at her lack of recollection. 'It's better to let your memory come back naturally, on its own. If you're told anything at all, then that won't happen.'

'So where is this friend of yours?'

'Right here...' Rafael told her, bronzed forearms tensing as he lifted something up and deposited it on the bed.

Totally bemused, Serena realised that she was staring at a carrycot, and inside, dressed in soft blue cotton, tiny feet bare, lay a small baby.

'Oh! He's *gorgeous*!' she exclaimed, her full mouth breaking into a smile of delight. Automatically she leaned forward, wanting to pick him up, then froze, unsure of what Rafael's response might be.

'You think so?'

Rafael's reaction was not at all what she had expected. There was a new and disturbing tension in his tone, one that jarred sharply, scraping over Serena's nerves and setting them sharply on edge.

'Of course I do! Wouldn't anyone…?'

Her words faded as, alerted by the sound of her voice, the baby stirred suddenly. His legs kicked sharply, small fists waving in the air, and his closed lids lifted, wide dark eyes looking directly into hers. Her breath suddenly caught in her throat as she felt an involuntary kick of response.

'What's his name?' she managed on a dry, painful croak.

A faint thatch of fine black hair fuzzed the baby's scalp. The black hair and something about the shape of the child's face reminded her strongly of the man beside her. The man whose image had haunted her thoughts by day, disturbed her sleep at night in heated, shockingly erotic dreams that she had woken from to find her heart still racing, her hair damp with sweat.

'His full name is Antonio Felipe Martinez Cordoba.'

Cordoba. There it was. The confirmation she had been dreading. How had this happened to her? How could this man, whom she had known for only a few days, have such an effect on her that it mattered so much to think that he might already be in a relationship? That he had fathered a child with another woman.

'What a mouthful.'

She concentrated her attention on the baby as she spoke, putting out a tentative finger to stroke one waving hand, a smile escaping her as she saw the way his little fist closed round it, clutching hard. And in that moment it was as if the little boy's hand had curled around her heart as well, taking it prisoner as it was flooded with an unexpected and totally overwhelming rush of love for this small, vulnerable being.

'A big name for such a little scrap.'

'I call him Tonio.'

'That suits him.' She bent forward, smiling into the child's wide eyes, the red-gold curtain of her hair falling round her oval face, forming a shield from Rafael's watchful gaze. 'He's yours?'

His wordless murmur went unheeded as her thoughts leapt on to the next logical connection.

'I didn't know you were married.'

'I'm not.' His unexpected response brought her head round in a rush, brown eyes widening in shock. 'Never have been, even though I came close to it once.'

'Then Tonio. He's a—a—love-child?'

Her heart was doing crazy things inside her chest: beating way too fast and twisting, practically turning somersaults, so that she was unable to breathe. Not married didn't mean not committed, and after all what greater commitment was there between two people than the fact that they had a child together?

'A love-child?' Rafael's beautifully shaped mouth twisted cynically on the word. 'There are those who would call him something far less complimentary.'

'But if you and his mother are together...'

'No!' It came forcefully, almost violently, and those brilliant golden eyes blazed with fierce rejection of her statement. 'Tonio's mother and I are not, as you so tactfully put it, "together".'

Serena's heart, which had started to slow down, to return to its natural rhythm, lurched painfully at the sudden change in his tone.

Somehow, without quite knowing how, she had overstepped whatever careful lines he drew around his personal life. The man she had grown accustomed to over the past few days had vanished and the person she had privately nicknamed the Spanish Inquisitor, the man who had so upset and frightened her at their first meeting, was back.

'I—I'm sorry. I didn't mean to pry.'

Thoroughly unnerved, she snatched her hand away from

the baby's grasp, suddenly afraid to show her response to the child.

'I never...'

But she got no further. Furious at having his new-found toy so abruptly snatched from him, Tonio murmured a faint protest which then developed into a full-blooded howl, his little face screwing into a furious grimace, his cheeks flushed bright red.

'Oh, sweetheart, I'm sorry!' Serena's remorse was immediate, her fear of Tonio's father forgotten as she moved hastily to comfort the little boy.

Rafael was there before her, scooping the child out of his carrycot and gathering him close.

'Hush, *mi corazón*, hush,' he soothed huskily. 'All is well; you're safe.'

Serena's heart tightened again, her nerves tying themselves into hard, painful knots at the sight of the baby held so firmly against the strength and width of the hard wall of the man's chest. His small, vulnerable form seemed so much tinier, so delicate when contrasted with the arms that enclosed him, the long-fingered hand that curved lovingly around the delicate skull, supporting the tiny head.

Immediately all the loneliness and apprehension that had gripped her just before Rafael's arrival flooded back with a vengeance.

This was why, in spite of her initial fear of him, she had been so glad to see Rafael when he had appeared in her room on the second day after she had regained consciousness. No one else was likely to visit. There was no one she could turn to who could help her obtain the small necessities that would make her stay in hospital that bit more comfortable.

And Rafael hadn't needed to be asked. In fact he had arrived that first day with flowers, fruit, and a bag containing a selection of toiletries, all of the most luxurious brands, more expensive than anything she had ever been able to provide for herself. He had even thought to bring a couple of new nightdresses, guessing at her size with an accuracy that had frankly astonished and unnerved her. It spoke of an intimate knowledge of the female body that she found she didn't want to enquire into too closely.

'Keep them!' he had declared dismissively when she had protested at his generosity. 'They're only trifles—I can easily afford them.'

But just that morning she had learned that the nightdresses and toiletries were only part of it, that his generosity went much further than she had ever imagined. And that was something she could not let go unchallenged.

'Is it true that you have been paying all my bills?'

Rafael's proud head came up sharply, black brows drawing together over the tawny eyes that were suddenly wary, as if he had something he very definitely wanted to conceal.

'Who told you that?' he demanded in a voice that promised retribution on the person responsible just as soon as he found out.

'Oh, come on, Mr Cordoba!' Serena protested. 'I may have had an accident—a knock on the head—but I've not completely lost my mind!'

'I thought we agreed on Rafael,' he inserted coolly, in an obvious attempt to distract her from her line of questioning.

'We *agreed* on nothing! You instructed me to use your name, told me not to worry my pretty little head about anything…'

And, weak and vulnerable, she had done just that. She had accepted his presence in the hospital because the medical staff did, hadn't persisted with the questions that had been so subtly but effectively blocked because with her head still aching and her thoughts still whirling in confusion it was easier not to. She had simply assumed that Rafael Cordoba had some part in the time she couldn't remember, the moments just before or just after the accident, and so hadn't pressed the matter.

But not now. Now she couldn't believe that she had been

so foolish, so blindly, stupidly naïve. Now she wanted some answers.

'And it wasn't just a bang on the head,' Rafael continued imperturbably, moving to lay the baby back in his carrycot. 'You were very much out of it there for a while, and you were lucky to get away with only the injuries you had.'

'You don't have to tell me that!' Serena retorted swiftly.

She still felt cold inside just to recall the moment when, helped by a nurse, she had first managed to struggle out of her hospital regulation gown and into one of the new, pretty cotton ones Rafael had provided for her. She had been shocked and horrified to see the bruising that covered so much of her body, the scratches and cuts that marred the whiteness of her skin.

And that bruising had been on her face as well, when she had finally nerved herself to look in a mirror. Patched and ugly, in shades that blended from dark purple to a nasty, fading yellow, it had mottled her forehead and all down the right side of her cheek. It was the darkest, most obviously damaged area, just above her eye, that had made her shudder to think just how lightly she had escaped and what might have happened.

'But I'm feeling better now, and I'm able to think straight again. For a start, I'm in a private ward. And I'd have to be all sorts of a fool to think that the food I'm getting, the nursing care, the comfort that's been provided is the same as I'd be getting if I had just been taken in as ordinary Serena Martin, brought in unconscious off the street, with no one to help her. So I asked a few questions...'

That didn't please him at all. It was stamped all over his autocratic face, etched into every arrogant line of bone and muscle. And the way his sensual mouth tightened, obviously clamping down on some angry response, dried her throat uncomfortably so that she had to force herself to continue.

'I was told that I was receiving private medical care, and that you were footing the bill. Is this true?'

For the space of several taut and uncomfortable seconds, it looked as if he wasn't going to answer her. But then a disdainfully curt nod of his dark head admitted the truth.

'But *why*? Why should you, a complete stranger, do all this for me? That is, if you *are* the stranger you said you were.'

'And why the devil would I lie to you?'

Scorn blazed in his eyes, searing over her skin until she felt as if it had scoured off a much-needed protective layer. Instinctively she folded her arms around herself, suddenly feeling over-exposed.

Temporarily she had managed to blot out the fact that she was actually in a bedroom, however institutionalised, in her nightclothes, while this darkly devastating man was fully dressed beside her. But that look had ripped away the shield she had built around her.

'I—I don't know. I can't even begin to imagine. You say I'd never met you before, and yet you do so much for me.'

'I told you I could afford it.'

'I know what you told me!'

Serena flung out her arms in a wild gesture of rejection of his response, heedless of the way it made the slightly too large neckline of her nightdress gape, revealing the rich curves of her breasts.

'It's what you're *not* saying that's bothering me! I don't need to know that you're some wildly rich international banker or that the cost of my stay here is just chickenfeed to someone with your millions. I want to know exactly *why* you're involved in all this—and don't you dare say, All what?' she flung at him as he drew breath sharply, prior, she was sure, to doing just that.

In his turn, Rafael lifted his own hands in a gesture that surprised her by its apparent mood of concession. But the wry twist to his mouth, the distinct glint in his eyes, spoke of something else entirely.

'You are obviously feeling much better,' he murmured dryly. 'But the doctor believes...'

'Yes, I know that the doctor believes it's better to wait. That she wants me to remember on my own. But I'm not remembering, and it's doing my head in... It's making me feel worse, even more confused,' she amended hastily as he frowned his confusion, even his near-perfect grasp of English incapable of following the slang phrase. 'I feel like I'm going out of my mind. I'm frightened—'

Her voice broke unevenly on the last word, hot tears burning in her eyes, making them glisten brilliantly as she struggled to blink them back.

'Right now you seem like the only person I know in the entire world, but I don't really *know* you! I don't know a thing about you except the way you seem to have moved in here, taking over...'

'*Maldito sea!* I felt responsible.'

It was the last thing she had expected and it stopped her dead, her eyes wide and stunned, her soft mouth actually falling open a little in shock.

'You? Responsible? But how?'

The look he turned on her made her stomach quail nauseously. Suddenly she wished she'd never opened her big mouth.

'It was my car.'

'Your...'

Through the tumult of emotion inside her head she couldn't begin to interpret the inflexion he put on the words, the feeling behind them. But she couldn't stop herself from reacting purely instinctively, recoiling back against the pillow, all colour leaching from her face, one hand coming up to cover her trembling mouth.

'You—you were *driving*?'

'*Dios*, no! I wasn't even in England at the time, but my—' He caught himself up sharply, seeming to hunt for the right words. 'It was my car that was involved in the accident.'

'Your car...' Slowly Serena lowered her protective hand, sitting back up a little, but her face was still clouded with confusion. 'Was I driving?'

'No. You were a passenger.' It was curt to the point of rudeness, obviously deeply reluctant.

'Then what...? How...?'

'Miss Martin...' Rafael used cold formality to freeze her out, stop her questioning in its tracks. 'May I remind you that I have been instructed not to give you the full facts about your accident? Doctor's orders, I believe you say.'

But now she was really worried. Being left to remember in her own time was one thing. This dreadful feeling that something was being kept from her because it would be too upsetting to know it quite another.

'But why? Did something awful happen? Who was the driver? Where is he—she—now?'

'Miss Martin—Serena...'

'*Rafael!*' It was wrenched from her, her state of mind too disturbed to notice the way she had used his Christian name as she lurched forward, half out of the bed, to grab hold of his hand and clutch at it hard. 'Please!'

For the space of perhaps two dozen long drawn-out, heart-thudding seconds he hesitated, obviously thinking hard. With his hooded eyes looking down into her own darkly shadowed ones, she saw him come to a decision, change his mind, rethink and change it again.

'*Please!*' she repeated, knowing intuitively that he had decided against her. 'I need to know.'

His sigh was a blend of exasperation and unwilling resignation.

'Serena—' he said at last. 'The driver... he did not survive the crash.'

'Oh, *no!*'

It was the worst she had imagined. The only thing that really explained his reluctance to speak. No, perhaps the worst thing was the way she was feeling—or rather not feeling. She couldn't even remember who had been driving the car, so she didn't know what she *should* be feeling.

'Who was he? Did I know him?'

But Rafael's face had closed up, heavy lids and long, luxuriant lashes hiding his eyes and his thoughts from her.

'That is for you to say.'

'Oh, that's not fair!'

But, 'doctor's orders' he had said, and he meant to abide by those orders, no matter what it did to her.

'I must have done, mustn't I? I mean—I was there with him—in the car. I wouldn't have got into a car with a stranger.'

She looked into his face, seeking a response that would help her, but finding only that stony-faced, blanked-off expression that made her think fearfully of the unseeing, frozen faces of the statues of Ancient Greece, carved from cold, unyielding marble.

'I *wouldn't*!' For some reason she felt the need to repeat it, to emphasise the importance of what she had said. 'I'm not that sort of a girl.'

He didn't say a word, but some change in his face, a movement of his head, an expression in those burning eyes, a momentary lift of one black brow that he couldn't quite control, seemed to question the truth of her assertion.

'You don't believe me?'

Angry now, she could no longer stay still. Swinging her legs out of bed, she got to her feet, snatching up the calf-length robe that matched her nightdress and pulling it on, belting it firmly around her slim waist with a rough, jerky movement that betrayed her inner feelings.

This was better. At least her slender height gave her the ability to look him in the eyes, even if he was still some five or so inches above her five-feet-nine.

'How dare you? You have no right to sit in judgement on me when you don't even know me—if that is the truth.'

'I had never set eyes on you in my life until the first day

I came to this hospital and saw you lying unconscious in that bed.'

'Then—then you can't tell me what I was doing at the time of the accident or just before it and why.'

Her delicate toes curling on the soft carpet, Serena shifted uncomfortably from one foot to another. She didn't want to think of Rafael standing beside her bed, looking down at her unconscious form from that imperious height. Just the thought of those cold eagle's eyes watching everything about her, judging, assessing, when she was utterly defenceless, unaware even of his presence, made her blood chill in her veins.

'You can't know anything about me—who I am or what I am—so you'll have to take my word for it that I'm just not that kind of woman.'

'You may believe that you were not that sort of woman—'

He bit off the sentence swiftly, but not quite quickly enough. Serena pounced on that revealing change of tense.

'*Were* not?' she repeated shakily. 'Were? What does that mean? What do you know that you aren't telling me?'

But he wouldn't meet her eyes. Instead he turned to where little Tonio still lay, sleeping peacefully.

'I have to leave,' he said, not even attempting to hide the fact that he was deliberately ignoring her anxious questions. 'Tonio will need feeding...'

'No! You can't do this to me! I won't let you!'

The sidelong glance he turned in her direction was one of supreme indifference. I can do exactly as I wish, it declared, as clearly as if he had spoken. And you can do nothing to stop me.

Oh, couldn't she?

Just as Rafael looped the handles of the carrycot over one strong hand she slipped past him, heading for the doorway and positioning herself just in front of it.

'I mean it!' she declared, praying that her vehemence hid every sign of the uncertainty that nagged at her.

'Serena...' Her name was threaded through with a note of ominous warning, one she knew she would be wise to heed, but she couldn't bring herself to give up the fight so easily.

'No. I won't let you go until you tell me. It's my life, I have a right to know!'

No, defiance was the wrong approach. It was only hardening his resolve. She could see that in the set of his jaw, the cold light in his eyes, the way they had narrowed, dangerously assessing. Hastily she rethought her plan of campaign.

'Rafael, please... ' she cajoled, carefully adjusting her tone, making it soft and pleading, totally unlike the challenge of moments before.

'Serena, don't do this... '

Are you sure you know what you're doing? a small, nervous voice questioned at the back of her mind. Are you sure that you really want to know?

'No!'

Stubbornly she pushed the weak thoughts away, refusing to let them take root. If she gave in to Rafael now, if she let him go without answering her, then she would have lost her chance for ever. If he defeated her once, he would always be able to do so again.

'Please—you don't know what it's been like! I've lain awake at nights trying and trying to remember, but it's all just a blank—a big, gaping black hole where that day should be. Can you imagine how that feels—how frightening it is?'

'Madre de Dios!'

Rafael dropped the handles of the carrycot and raked both hands through the shining luxuriance of his black hair in a gesture so expressive of burning exasperation that Serena couldn't hold back a smile at the knowledge that she was getting through to him at last.

'You will regret this.'

It was a flat statement of fact, not a threat, and that was

what firmed her resolve, making her even more set on continuing.

'I'll regret it even more if I don't find out what you're talking about. This is my past—my life! How can I ever hope to move on, go forward, if I don't know what's behind me?'

Rafael's only answer was another outburst of explosive Spanish, but at the end of it he flung up his hands in a gesture of defeat.

'All right, you asked for it! And perhaps it is best that you know the truth. That date you gave... '

'It wasn't right? I was unconscious longer than I believed?'

'On the contrary. In all but one detail the date was perfectly correct. The right day, the right month...'

'But...' She had to force the word out in a hoarse, tight-throated croak, because it was obvious that there had to be a 'but'.

'But it was a year early.'

'Early? I don't understand.'

'The date you gave to the doctor was the right day, right month *last year*. And you are not twenty-three, but twenty-*four*. The accident, the injury to your head, left you with partial amnesia. It's not just the last few days that you can't remember. You've lost a year of your life.'

CHAPTER THREE

YOU'VE lost a year of your life. A year of your life. A year.

The words Rafael had flung at her formed a tormenting, thudding refrain inside her skull whenever she wasn't thinking about anything else.

And she had too much time to think. Nothing held her attention; nothing distracted her from the appalling fact that she could not manage to come to terms with.

In the daytime she could try to read, or watch television, but inevitably she had found it was impossible to concentrate. She would find that she had been staring blankly at the screen or a page on which not a single word had registered, and all the time those impossible, incredible words had swung round and round in her mind, beating at her brain with a bruising sense of horror. But the nights, in the silence and the darkness, were much, much worse.

You've lost a year of your life.

How was it possible? How could this have happened? More importantly, *why* had it happened? How could she simply forget about a year that she had lived? How could something wipe out twelve months, three hundred and sixty-five days of her existence, destroying it and leaving not a trace of anything behind?

'No!'

She cried the word aloud in an attempt to drive away the demons of fear and panic that seemed to prowl around her, hidden in the shadows, tormenting her.

She wouldn't give in to this, she vowed. Wouldn't go down under the waves of horror that threatened to engulf her. She would fight them with everything at her disposal. Her past couldn't stay buried for ever. Her memories would have to emerge some day, and she would do everything she could to make sure that day came just as soon as possible.

Not that she had much to go on. Her few belongings were no help. The clothes she had been wearing at the time of the accident had been ruined, but she was assured that they had been strictly anonymous, inexpensive chainstore items, with no distinguishing marks on them at all, ditto her shoes. And the small, battered brown leather handbag that had been picked up at the crash scene held only a purse containing just a few pounds in cash, a comb, a packet of tissues and a key. That was all.

'If only there'd been a diary, or something with an address on it!' Serena had wailed when Dr Greene had assured her that nothing had been taken or hidden from her.

'It's been left exactly as it was handed to us, I'm afraid. The police have investigated that address in Yorkshire that you gave us, but it turned out to be a dead end.'

'No help at all?'

The doctor shook her dark head, grey eyes sympathetic.

'I'm sorry, no. It was just one bedsit out of a dozen or so in an old house that's usually rented out to students. Apparently when you lived there everyone who shared the house with you was in their final year. They've all moved on, far and wide, and very few of them even bothered to leave forwarding addresses.'

'And Leanne?'

Leanne was someone she'd remembered. A friend from her student days. Her best friend.

'I went to university late, because my mother was so ill,' she'd told the doctor, sadness clouding her eyes at the memory. 'She had ovarian cancer and I postponed my starting date because I wanted to stay at home and nurse her. So I was twenty-two when I started my course. It seemed that everyone else was so much younger than me, and I didn't really make any friends until I moved into Alban Road. That was where I met Leanne.'

'You said she'd emigrated to Australia?'

'That's right. She was engaged to an Australian doctor and she was going to live with him after the wedding.'

Serena had been invited to the wedding, she knew that much. And she was sure she would have gone. There was no way she would have missed her friend's big day. But, try as she might, she couldn't recall anything about it. It seemed that the start of Leanne's marriage marked the end of the lifetime she could remember.

'But Australia's a huge place when you've no idea where to start looking. Worse than the proverbial needle in a haystack. I would have had her address somewhere; I know I would! But I've no idea where it is now.'

That address must be wherever she had lived in the year since she had left Yorkshire. Because she had learned that much at least. Something had happened to her; something so important or traumatic that she had thrown up her university course and...

And what? Lying awake in the darkness, Serena thumped her pillow in a rage of impotent frustration. The answer to that question was lost, along with her memory.

'So what do I do now?'

Because she had to do something. The injuries she'd received in the crash were well on their way to mending, the cuts all but healed, even the worst of the bruises fading away completely. Physically, there was nothing to keep her in the hospital any longer.

'Oh, I don't think you need to worry about that.' Dr Greene smiled. 'Mr Cordoba has it all in hand.'

'Just what are you up to now?'

Rafael had barely had time to get through the door into her room that evening before Serena rounded on him, flinging the furious question into his face.

'Up to? My dear Miss Martin, precisely what are you talking about?'

'You know perfectly well what I'm talking about!'

Serena faced him defiantly across the room, black coffee-coloured eyes flashing fire, her chin up, every inch of her slender body stiff with rejection of his high-handed way of behaving. He hadn't brought Tonio with him this time, she noted gratefully, knowing that the little boy would distract her from the questions she had to ask.

'And I'm not your "dear Miss Martin"! I'm not your "dear" anything! You can't just move in and take over my life.'

'And how—exactly—am I supposed to be doing that?'

The coolly drawled question incensed her, as did the slow, indolently assessing way those brilliant eyes swept over her, narrowing slightly as they considered the oatmeal-coloured loose trousers and cream tee shirt she was wearing. The insolent sensuality of the survey made her heart kick against her ribs, her breathing catch for a second.

'The clothes suit you well.'

'Don't change the subject!' Serena exploded, bitterly conscious of the fact that if it had not been for Rafael she would have had nothing to wear, or at least something far less expensive and stylish.

'This is my *life* we're talking about. And you can't take people's lives and assess them as if they were some sheet of figures you've been handed to check through. You can't just add up the income and the outgoings, take away the number you first thought of, decide if it's worth the investment you were planning on, and then draw a nice neat line under everything—done—finished—sorted out!'

Rafael's laughter had a disturbing edge to it, one that took his response to a point a long, long way from true amusement and turned it into something that sent a trickle of icy apprehension sliding down her spine.

'Who the devil thought to name you *Serena* with a temper like that?' he murmured sardonically, moving to throw his long body down into the easy chair that stood beside the window. 'But then I suppose I should have expected it from...'

'From what?' Serena demanded when he let the sentence trail off unfinished, his eye apparently caught by something in the street outside. 'You should have expected it from *whom*?'

She regretted the angry emphasis she had put on the last word as Rafael's proud head snapped round again, his beautiful eyes no longer warm with any degree of amusement but cold and sharp as if carved from golden ice.

'From someone with your hair colouring,' he told her curtly. 'Fiery hair, fiery temper—isn't that true?'

'I—' Serena began indignantly, but, meeting a flashing warning glance that made her toes curl in fearful response, she hastily gulped down the irritable protest, forcing herself to begin again.

'Believe it or not, I'm not usually like this. As a matter of fact, I'm usually pretty equable. Oh, don't you dare look at me like that!' she flung at him when the twist of his mouth, a tilt of his head questioned her assertion without words.

'I rest my case,' he murmured with silky cynicism.

'If you must know, *you* make me lose my temper! You drive me to it.'

'And why is that, do you think?'

'Why...?'

Totally at a loss, Serena could only shake her head. Why did he affect her in this way? Why was her mental equilibrium so precariously balanced whenever he was around that just a look, a word, a gesture was enough to throw it out completely?

She had never thought of herself as an emotionally volatile person, flying off the handle at the slightest provocation, yet somehow when she was with Rafael she became as uncontrolled as a weathercock, swinging this way and that in response to his passing mood.

'Because you have to be the most provoking man I've ever

come across. And the way you've behaved is a decidedly excessive reaction simply because I was hurt in your car.'

'I was brought up always to meet my responsibilities.'

Like Tonio. The thought flashed into Serena's mind in a moment. Rafael had never explained just what had happened to the baby's mother, but it was patently clear that he had no intention of being an absentee father. Or had he just moved in on the poor woman, as he was now doing with Serena herself, taking control, *taking over*, no matter what anyone else wanted?

'There's meeting responsibilities and there's trampling other people underfoot!'

Rafael's exaggeratedly patient sigh brought her up short, painfully aware of the way it warned her that his grip on his temper was loosening rapidly.

'Are you going to rant at me like this for the rest of the evening?' he enquired in a voice laced with acid. 'Or do you ever intend to enlighten me as to just what is bugging you?'

'Isn't it obvious? The thing that's "bugging" me—' Serena matched his satire word for word '—is that you think you can just make plans for my future and I'll fall in with them as soon as you snap your fingers. So when were you going to tell me? Today? Tomorrow? When it suited you? Or were you just going to present me with a *fait accompli* and say, This, and this, and this is what's going to happen. If you don't like it—tough!?'

The fact that Rafael didn't honour her outburst with a reply, but simply continued to regard her stonily, brilliant eyes carefully blanked off, told her all she needed to know. When he looked down his aristocratic nose at her like that, she felt like some out-of-control two-year-old indulging in a petulant tantrum in front of a decidedly bored and critical parent. And that feeling only incensed her more, driving her to rush on without waiting for him to answer.

'That was it, wasn't it? I wasn't going to get a choice. So, tell me, what exactly did you have in mind for my future?'

'I thought you could come and live with me.'

'*What?*'

Unable to believe she had heard right, Serena shook her head disbelievingly.

'Live with *you*! No way!'

'And what else do you propose to do?' he came back at her swiftly, abandoning his indolent pose and pushing himself to his feet in one easy, lithe movement. 'You have no money, nowhere to live, no way of supporting yourself...'

'Do you think I'm not aware of that?'

The fact that only a short time before she had detailed exactly those points to herself did nothing to ease her edgy state of mind. If anything, it made her feel worse.

'So you had some alternative to suggest?'

The Spanish Inquisitor was back, with a vengeance. Uneasily Serena took a step or two backwards, edging away from his imposing height, the sheer physical force of his presence.

His movement had brought a wave of scent to her nostrils. The clean, crisp tang of some light cologne he wore, and underneath it the deeper, muskier, more intensely personal scent of his body. A perfume that brought all her senses onto red alert, making her head swim, hazing her thoughts.

'Not yet,' she hedged warily.

'Then what is wrong with coming to live with me until you decide what you want to do?'

'You know what's wrong with it!'

'Enlighten me.'

It seemed that the more her temper grew, the more impassive and withdrawn Rafael became, until she felt as if she was banging her fists hard against an unyielding brick wall in a vain attempt to get through to him.

'I know what you want—what you're thinking!'

'Oh, so now you're a mind-reader. So tell me, Señorita Martin, just what it is that you believe I want from you?'

'I—you…' she floundered, unable to find a way to put her thoughts into words.

He must know what she meant. He *had* to!

Wasn't he aware of what was between them? Couldn't he feel it, sense it in the air around them, like the heavy, lowering build-up in the atmosphere just before a violent electrical storm? That the storm hadn't broken yet was more by luck than good management.

Away from the restricting confines of her present surroundings, it could be a different story entirely. Just the thought of moving into his house made all the tiny hairs on the back of her neck stand up, her skin prickle with tension.

'Are you going to say what you mean?' Rafael demanded sharply. 'Or are you going to stand there all day, throwing out veiled hints because you don't have the nerve to be honest?'

Not have the nerve! Serena thought indignantly. Right, he'd asked for it.

'I think you have strong sexual feelings for me!'

There! It was out now, and no matter what she did she couldn't wish it back. Emboldened by his silence, by the fact that nothing had blown up in her face, she rushed on.

'Th-that you want me in your bed. I can see it in your eyes, in the way that you look at me when you think I'm not looking. Sometimes I can hear it in your voice too. And don't tell me I'm imagining things because…'

'I wouldn't dream of it,' Rafael inserted silkily, taking her breath away. 'Why should I deny something that must be obvious to anyone who looks at me? I'd be all sorts of a fool even to try.'

His voice had deepened, dropping a couple of octaves, becoming huskily sensual so that it coiled round her like warm, perfumed smoke.

'I don't want to try.'

She hadn't seen him move, but suddenly he was close, so close. His awesome height and strength was intimidating, making her breath catch in her throat. If she wanted to, she could reach out and touch him, feel that warm velvet skin beneath her fingertips, slide her fingers through the black silk of his hair.

If she wanted to! Serena almost laughed aloud at the thought.

Oh, she wanted to! She wanted it so much that it was like a pain in her heart. But she didn't *dare*. Some inner sixth sense warned her that if she gave in to the yearning, the need that clenched in her stomach, coiled round her body, then the repercussions of that simple act would be cataclysmic. It would be a case of light the blue touchpaper and stand well back. And when the smoke and debris of the resulting explosion cleared there would be nothing left that she recognised, no trace of the world she had known, the life she had lived.

'You're a very beautiful woman, Serena Martin. So beautiful that you twist my guts into knots, make me ache to possess you. From the moment I saw you I had one thought in my mind...'

'One th-thought?' Serena could only echo his words, her mind refusing to function so that she could form any of her own.

'In the instant that I saw you there, in that hospital bed, I knew I could never rest until I'd held you, kissed you like this...'

Rafael suited actions to the words, reaching out and folding his arms around her, gathering her close. And she went into his embrace like a sleepwalker, feeling as if this had been meant, as if it had been ordained from the moment she had been born. She had no thought of resistance, of asking why. She only knew that this was how it had to be.

So when that arrogant dark head lowered, she automatically raised hers to meet it, her mouth already softening for his kiss.

But when that kiss came, it had nothing of gentleness.

Instead it was as fierce and demanding as the touch of a flame, searing over her skin, scorching her senses, taking, plundering right to the depths of her soul. A raw, shaken cry was driven from her as she swayed on her feet, her arms reaching up to clasp around his neck, slender fingers digging into the powerful muscles that corded his shoulders, clinging on for support.

The whole of her mind was a red, heated haze, burning away all trace of coherent thought under a blazing inferno of sensation. Every inch of her skin seemed to be suffused with the stinging pins and needles of heightened awareness, yearning for his touch, and deep down, at the most feminine centre of her body, a pulsing hunger made her stir restlessly against the hard power of his lean frame.

On a groan of hunger Rafael brought his hands up to fasten on her hips, bronzed fingers stroking the curving line of her waist, the softness of her buttocks, pressing her closer against him. There was no escaping the heated, swollen pressure that indicated the power of the passion that gripped him, the hungry need for her body that he couldn't conceal.

Wild, crazy images filled her mind. Images of walking, step by step, backwards towards the bed, taking this man with her. Of tumbling down onto the peach-coloured bedspread, imprisoned under the heavy, glorious weight of him. Of his hands following the example of her own and tugging at her clothing, impatiently pushing aside the unwanted garments that came between his touch and her naked flesh. Of...

But there her imagination failed, short-circuited by the sheer mind-blowing reality of her fantasy made fact.

Rafael's strong, tanned fingers had pushed the cream tee shirt away from the waistband of her trousers and were insinuating themselves underneath the fine cotton, scorching her skin where they touched, drawing heated erotic circles as they moved slowly, inexorably upwards. And the reality was so much better than anything her imagination had invented

Better, and more pleasurable, and more arousing. Reality

made her heart race out of control, her skin sting with excitement, as his touch slid over her narrow ribcage to close over the slight curves of her breasts, cupping and supporting their warm weight.

'Rafael...' His name was a choked cry, smothered under the pressure of yet another, even more demanding kiss.

Answering the hunger that suffused her, she pushed her hands up between their bodies, pulling roughly, urgently on the buttons that fastened his shirt, yanking them apart in her impatience to be able to touch him in return. The feel of his hot flesh drew a deep, ragged sigh of satisfaction from her, a sigh that blended into a little gasp of pleasure as his hands moved against her breast again. That gasp became a moan as the warm, hard pads of his thumbs unerringly found the sensitive points of her nipples and set up a slow, circular motion that made every nerve waken into screaming need.

She was oblivious to the fact that the door was still partially open, to the sound of movement in the corridor outside. The warmth of the sun coming through the window at her back was just another sensual delight in a bombardment of such pleasures that made her head spin out of control. It wasn't until a voice spoke, just beyond the door, that any sense of reality impinged on her at all.

'...I believe Mr Cordoba's in there right now.'

At the sound of his name, Rafael snapped up his dark head sharply, his stance that of a disturbed predator, every muscle taut, his breathing ragged and uneven, listening intently. Only when the owner of the voice moved away down the corridor did he shake off the wary mood, looking down into Serena's dazed brown eyes with a twist to his mouth that was half-rueful, half-amused.

'This is neither the time nor the place for this,' he told her, releasing her from the seductive imprisonment of his hold and stepping back a couple of paces, smoothing down the ruffled tee shirt as he did so.

From being the ardent, demanding caress of a lover, his

touch was now all distance and matter of factly businesslike, the contrast between the two moods so sharp that it drew a cry of protest from her.

'Rafael...' she began, but he shook his head to silence her, raking both hands through the dark disarray of his hair to smooth down the disorder her clutching fingers had created.

'Not here, not now,' he insisted, with a cold precision that fell onto her heated skin like drops of ice, shattering the glowing mood of moments before. 'Not ever, if I am wise.'

'Not...' Serena choked on the words, unable to believe what she had heard. What had he said? *Why* had he said it?

Her aroused body still sang in excited expectation, the heightened rate of her pulse still sending the blood speeding through her veins. But slowly, unwillingly, a terrible sense of let-down was creeping over her, cooling the warmth of her skin, making her ache in frustration for the delights she had known and that were now denied her. She felt as if she had been reaching for the stars, only to have them snatched away from her with brutal cruelty.

'N-not now?'

She couldn't say the other phrase she thought she had heard. Couldn't make her tongue form the words 'not ever'.

'Miss Martin—Serena...'

In the blink of an eye, it seemed, Rafael had himself once more completely under control. His appearance was near perfect again, his hair smooth, his shirt fastened, his tie restored to order around the tanned column of his throat. And it seemed that in those moments he had also erased every trace of all that had happened between them as easily as he had wiped away the faint trace of lipstick that had transferred itself from her mouth to his.

'Forgive me. That should never have happened. I apologise for my actions.'

The stiff formality of his words, his stance, stabbed at her harshly. There was a nasty, bitter taste in her mouth and her stomach roiled queasily. How could he take something that had been so—so special, so wonderful, and turn it into a monstrous mistake, all in the space of a moment?

'There's no need to apologise...'

Her tone matched his in its stiffness, in the distance she deliberately put between them. Unconsciously, she mirrored his actions of moments before, straightening her clothes, stroking down her hair.

'I wasn't exactly forced. I was well aware of what was happening.'

'Serena!'

His use of her name was a sound of pure exasperation.

'You have no memory of the past year. Anything could have happened in that time. Until you know what there was in those twelve months, who you were with, you can't make any decision about the future.'

'Who I was with—do you know something?'

She watched in something close to despair as his face closed up, heavy lids hooding the brilliant eyes, hiding his thoughts from her.

'If you did, you wouldn't say anything, right?' she continued despondently. 'Don't tell me—doctor's orders.'

'I had no right to touch you.'

'And if I wanted to give you that right?'

She knew the answer before the question had even left her lips, anticipated the unyielding shake of his head that took away the last grain of hope she had left.

'There can be nothing between us while your memories remain elusive.' Cold and inflexible, his words had the force of a slashing steel blade. 'Nothing at all.'

'Then you—you won't want me to come and live with you?'

'On the contrary. I still think my original plan is for the best.'

'Your—your original plan? But if you don't want me...'

The look he turned on her was pure scorn, blazing over her skin with the force of a laser beam.

'*Madre de Dios!* You believed *that* was the reason I invited you to my home?'

He was pure Spaniard now. Tall and arrogant as any matador, head held high, strong jaw set, his handsome features forming a mask of cold anger, furiously rejecting the implications behind her question. She had insulted him, Serena reflected miserably. Insulted and appalled him and although he hadn't actually moved away from her she knew that he had mentally taken several major steps away from her.

'I'm sorry...' she began miserably, but he brushed aside her interjection with the brusque flick of his hand she had seen him use before.

'That was not it at all. I was thinking of Tonio...'

'*Tonio!*' Serena almost choked on the word. 'What has Tonio to do with this?'

'Everything,' Rafael snapped. 'I am a businessman, Serena. I have interests in England, Spain—all over Europe. I work long hours—I could be called away at any time to deal with some crisis. Tonio is just a baby. He needs love and care, someone who can be there with him...'

At last Serena saw the direction in which his thoughts were heading.

'Someone like me.'

A swift, curt inclination of his head acknowledged the accuracy of her guess.

'You want me to be some sort of nanny...'

Her voice shook on the words, but whether in laughter or distress she had no idea. She felt perilously close to both, hot tears burning in her eyes so that she blinked hard, determined not to let them fall.

This was what he had meant all along. How could she have been so foolishly naïve? She had thought that he was attracted to her, that he hadn't been able to resist her. She had believed that he had invited her to stay with him because he wanted to get to know her better. Instead, he had considered the problem—hers and his—quite coldly and come up with a purely pragmatic solution.

She needed a home. Rafael could provide one. He needed someone to care for his child and he had decided that that was a service *she* could offer in return for her board and lodging. The idea of his wanting her in any other way had had nothing to do with it.

'But I don't know anything about looking after a baby!'

'You will learn.'

Once again her objections were dismissed peremptorily.

'And I saw the look on your face when I brought him in here. I have no intention of leaving him with some woman for whom this is a job and nothing more. I want someone who would put him first always.'

Someone who didn't have a life, Serena reflected bitterly, linking the fingers of both hands together and staring down at them in order to hide the expression in her eyes from him. She had nowhere else to go, no one to turn to. He knew that, and had used it ruthlessly against her. He might have couched it in terms of offering her a job, helping her, but he knew only too well that he held all the cards in his hands.

But then she thought of Tonio, of his big, unblinking eyes, and the way his tiny hand had closed around her finger, and her heart clenched on a wave of emotion.

The baby was Rafael's trump card. He must have seen her face when she had looked down at him, the tenderness she hadn't been able to disguise. In the first moment she had seen him something deep and primitive had tugged at her heart. There was no way she could turn her back on the motherless infant, and Rafael knew that.

'You need a home, a place to live while you convalesce and regain your strength, and Tonio needs a nanny. You can live in my home; there is more than enough room for everyone. I have a housekeeper who will serve as a chaperon if you should feel the need of one. I will pay you a decent wage. It's an arrangement that will suit us all.'

'It seems very fair.'

It was a perfectly sensible arrangement, Serena told herself drearily. And perhaps, if he had suggested it yesterday, she might have seen it as the answer to all her problems. If he had suggested it before he had taken her in his arms. Before he had kissed her in a way that had changed their relationship for ever.

But he *had* held her. He had kissed her. And as a result of the dreams she had allowed herself to indulge in, just for a moment, what he now offered her could only ever be second best.

'Then you agree?'

Did she have any choice?

'Serena?' Rafael prompted hardly. 'I need an answer.'

And there was really only one she could give him. Slowly, reluctantly, she nodded.

'I agree.'

It was obviously the response he had expected. The swift, brusque nod of his dark head told her he had never anticipated anything else. Pushing back the cuff of his crisp white shirt, he consulted the slim watch that he wore on his wrist, gold against the bronze of his skin.

'I have to go now,' he said, brisk and businesslike once more, the matter settled to his satisfaction, his mind already moving on to other things. 'But I'll be back in the morning. Dr Greene says that she expects to discharge you then, so I will collect you as soon as she has made the final decision... Around ten-thirty, then?'

'Ten-thirty.'

But as he turned and headed for the door she found she could no longer hold back. All the feelings, all the hunger he had woken in her came flooding back with such force that before she quite realised what was happening she had opened her mouth and spoken impetuously.

'Rafael!'

The tone of her voice brought him to an abrupt halt, turning on his heel and swinging round to face her.

'What is it?'

'You—you said that—that while I still had no memory then there could be nothing at all between us... But what if things changed? If my memory came back—and I knew all about myself? What would happen then?'

Rafael's breath hissed in between his teeth as he considered his answer, and the momentary pause made her heart clench in something close to panic inside her chest.

'If that happened,' he said slowly, golden eyes burning into hers, holding her unmoving. 'If you remembered, then things would be so very different. In that case, *belleza*, all bets would very definitely be off.'

CHAPTER FOUR

SERENA stared out of her bedroom window, struggling to take in what she saw. The contrast with the modest size and facilities of her hospital room, comfortable though it had been, could not have been greater.

There was enough room here to house a family of twelve, an army of nannies, and then some more! The gardens stretched out on all sides, making it impossible to believe they were only a few miles from London. And this was only Rafael's 'English base'. The place where he stayed when business commitments brought him to Britain. His family home, he had told her was in Almeria. And he also had an apartment in Madrid.

So what was she doing here, in the middle of all this luxury? How had Serena Martin, a girl from the Yorkshire Dales whose one ambition had been to study History at university and then perhaps teach, ended up living with a Spanish millionaire, ostensibly acting as nanny to his baby son?

'I told you, I want someone who will care for Tonio,' he had declared impatiently when, in the car on the way here, she had raised the question that had fretted at her all night. 'All the qualifications in the world count for nothing if there is no real affection. There are too many horror stories in the papers these days. I prefer to go with my own judgement.'

'And your judgement says precisely what about me? What can I offer your son?'

'Two arms to hold him safely, a soft voice to soothe him when he cries. Someone to distract him when he is restless...'

'Any woman could do that!' Serena protested. 'Why does it have to be me?'

'Are you saying you don't want the job?' Rafael questioned sharply, his hands tightening on the steering wheel.

'No, of course I'm not saying that! It's just that I don't see why you are so determined to have *me*...'

The sudden realisation of how ambiguously her words could be interpreted, the awareness of the knowing glint in Rafael's eyes as he slanted a swift, assessing glance at her face, closed her throat on the rest of the sentence. Unable to continue, she could only subside back into her seat as Rafael changed gear smoothly and pressed his foot down firmly on the accelerator.

'You suit me, Serena Martin,' he said calmly above the roar of the engine. 'And I think you'll suit Tonio.'

A sudden thought occurred to her and she turned in her seat, her confusion clear on her face.

'How did you get to hear about the accident? I mean, did they contact you in Spain?'

Would a man of his standing, someone with his business commitments, actually travel all that way to sort out the chaos left by an accident involving his car?

'I was already on my way to England.'

Rafael's fine profile, etched against the car window, seemed to have tightened sharply, drawing his skin taut across the powerful bones. His jaw had clenched, warning her that once again she had overstepped that invisible barrier that he had laid out around his personal life.

'I had an important meeting here that day. Instead I arrived to find the police on my doorstep, my—'

Unexpectedly he clashed the gears with an ugly grinding sound and gave vent to a curse in explosive Spanish.

'My car a write-off and you in a hospital bed, dead to the world.'

'I bet that pleased you.' Serena resorted to flippancy to hide her response to the cold shadow of tension that always slithered down her spine at the thought of his presence in the hospital room where she lay unconscious.

'I've had better days.' It was icy and flat, any emotion he was feeling carefully concealed. 'I... What is it?' he asked sharply as Serena gave a sudden gasp of horror, lifting her hands to her face in shock.

'The man who was driving the car. You said he died. Should I have gone to his funeral—or at least sent flowers—some message...?'

'The funeral was held five days after the accident.' Rafael's response was clipped and icy, his attention apparently on negotiating a roundabout. 'At a time when you were in no fit state to be going anywhere or doing anything. Besides, I very much doubt that his family would have appreciated your presence or any other gesture from you.'

There it was again, that worrying certainty that Rafael knew so much more than he was letting on. Serena shifted uneasily in her seat, fighting against the wave of near panic that swamped her at the thought that in some way her life was not her own. That this man had possession of the memories she couldn't recall.

'And why is that?' she said sharply. 'Are you saying I'd done something to offend them? That I wouldn't have been welcome?'

From some dark corner of her thoughts came the memory of Rafael in her hospital room saying, *You may believe you were not that sort of woman,* and the recollection made her stomach twist in nervous horror.

'You're not saying I had an affair with him! I couldn't have... Rafael, please tell me he wasn't married!'

'That would trouble you?'

'Of course it would! I would never knowingly have an affair with a married man—at least...'

Fear swamped her at the realisation that she couldn't say 'never' about the things she couldn't remember.

'Amnesia can be very wilful,' Dr Greene had told her. 'It isn't just the after-effects of a blow to the head. Sometimes what the patient has blotted out are the memories they can't bear to face up to. The things they don't *want* to recall.'

'No, I wouldn't.'

Fiercely she shook her head, refusing to accept that under any circumstances she would have gone so strongly against what she believed to be right.

'I *couldn't*!' This time her voice rang with conviction. 'He wasn't married, was he?'

For a long moment she thought he wasn't going to answer her as he concentrated on his driving with an intensity that she secretly doubted he needed. But then at last he shook his head slowly.

'He wasn't married,' he confirmed deeply.

'Thank God for that.'

Serena tried to relax back in her seat, but she couldn't be unaware of the way that Rafael's response had given her only half of the answer she needed. But she couldn't ask what her relationship had been with the car's driver. Or rather she could ask, but she knew only too well that she would get no answer if she did.

Rafael was determined to stick strictly to the doctor's instructions that she was to be left to regain her memory by herself, at her own pace. The few bits and pieces he had let slip had been given so reluctantly she had had to drag them out of him, and there was no point in pressing him any further. It would only make him clam up even more.

And so she kept quiet, saying nothing, as Rafael turned the car in at an imposing set of gates and headed up a sloping driveway bordered on either side by dense green shrubbery.

'Is this it?' Serena looked round her with interest. 'Oh, boy, it's going to take me an age to learn how to find my way around this place! It's huge!'

Huge and forbidding, she told herself as a shiver slid down her spine as if the sun had just gone behind a cloud. But a moment later she rethought.

No, it wasn't the house—that was an elegant Edwardian

building, warm and mellow in the afternoon sun, the rustle of the ivy that climbed up its walls the only sound in the silence. But something about the place, some unknown sensation she had picked up, made her heart beat suddenly with a terrible sense of dread, a premonition of something waiting for her just out of sight.

The feeling lingered at the back of her mind for the rest of the day, making her feel restless and unsettled, her unease aggravated by Rafael's withdrawn mood, the way he held himself at a distance, barely tossing a word in her direction. As a result she was grateful for the opportunity to concentrate her attention on Tonio, feeding him his bottle and then giving him his bath before he went to bed.

Bathtime was an absolute delight, she discovered, as the little boy kicked and splashed happily, chuckling in joy as the warm water showered all over her, soaking into her pale blue shirt and jeans.

'So just who is giving who a bath?' Rafael enquired dryly, having appeared unnoticed in the doorway while she was absorbed in a silly game of peek-a-boo from behind a rubber duck. 'You couldn't be any wetter if you'd got in there with him.'

'What's a bit of water?' Serena retorted, lifting Tonio from the bath and enfolding him in a fluffy white towel. 'I'll soon dry.'

'Yes, but will the room?' His golden-eyed gaze took in the puddles on the floor, the bubbles clinging to the tiled walls. But Serena was glad to see that the stern set of his face had softened and his smile actually warmed his eyes.

'Won't you tell me a little more about Tonio?' she said, patting the wriggling little body dry. 'If I'm to look after him, then I should know much more than just his name. How old is he, for a start?'

'He's not quite twelve weeks old. He was born on the ninth of June.'

'So young?'

Her voice shook on the words and she looked down into the wide, bright eyes of the child on her lap. Tonio was just a tiny scrap. How could his mother ever have given him up, even to his father? And how did she now feel, living without her baby son?

And how had Rafael ended up with sole custody of the baby? Wasn't it more often the case that a judge would award custody to the mother in such a case? Surely it would be better for a child so young to be with his mother in his early years?

'You sound nervous.' Rafael had caught the uncertainty in her voice. 'Exactly what is troubling you?'

'It's an awesome responsibility, looking after a child that small,' Serena hedged, not daring to let him in on the real direction of her thoughts. She concentrated fiercely on drying Tonio's feet, tickling the small pink toes to make him laugh so that she didn't have to look up into Rafael's face.

'You'll soon settle down into a routine. After all, Tonio's still too little to do much more than sleep and feed. He's not even on solids yet. Just so long as you're there when he cries and cuddle him and give him his bottle...'

'Does he have some special toy—something that he must always have with him when he sleeps?'

Rafael nodded. 'There's Conejo.'

'There's what?'

Serena turned to him in confusion.

'Conejo.'

Rafael's grin was slightly sheepish, thoroughly disarming. Just for a moment he looked years younger, almost boyish, and Serena felt the impact of that rather lopsided smile hitting home, finding a vulnerable spot in her heart and twisting it sharply.

This must be what he had looked like at the age of perhaps ten or so. Impish, slightly vulnerable and utterly irresistible. It would be the way Tonio would grow up too, becoming a small mirror image of his father in the future.

'Who or what is Conejo?' she managed to ask, struggling to smooth away the unevenness in her voice that was the result of a distinct fluttering of her heart in response to the devastating appeal of that smile, the enchanting and unexpected twinkle in those brilliant eyes, warming them and turning them to the rich colour of molten honey.

'A rather ugly hand-knitted bunny rabbit that Tonio absolutely adores. It has to be in his cot at night or heaven help us—no one gets any sleep.'

'I'll have to remember that. And I presume that *conejo* means rabbit in Spanish?' Was Tonio's mother Spanish? Serena couldn't help wondering.

'Exactly. If you've finished drying, hand him over and I'll get him dressed.'

It was a command, not a request, leaving Serena with no option but to obey, despite her reluctance to place the baby in Rafael's waiting arms. She had loved having Tonio on her knee, adored the feel of his soft skin, rosy pink from his bath, the sweet, clean baby smell of him, and felt disturbingly lost and bereft without the warmth of his small, sturdy body close by.

'You're very good with him,' she said, watching as Rafael pulled the navy blue sleepsuit onto the wriggling little boy. 'Not every man could cope with such a small baby.'

Once again Rafael's hard features softened perceptibly, the corners of his mouth curving into a smile.

'I always wanted children, though not quite as much as my mother and father dreamed of becoming grandparents. They dote on Tonio.'

'Any grandparent would. I'm surprised that you didn't want them to take care of him.'

'I wanted him here, with me.' Rafael snapped the last fastening shut and lifted Tonio once more, heading for the door. 'Bedtime for you, *gatito*.'

It was when the now drowsy baby had been settled contentedly in his cot and they were once more out on the landing that the memory of the uncomfortable feeling she had experienced on their arrival washed over Serena once again, driving her into impulsive speech.

'Was I ever here before?' she asked suddenly, her voice cracking on the words.

Rafael's dark head came round sharply, gleaming eyes narrowed in swift assessment.

'I don't know. I *do not* know,' he repeated emphatically when she turned sceptical eyes on him.

'And if you knew, you wouldn't tell.'

'And you know why.'

He was walking away from her as he spoke, his movement declaring without words that he believed the conversation was over.

'Oh, yes, I know why...doctor's orders...doctor's orders,' she chanted sarcastically, directing the words at the long, straight line of his back, which was all she could see of him. 'That's all I ever get parroted at me, every time...'

The words died on her lips as Rafael whirled round angrily. His spectacular eyes gleamed dangerously, his beautiful mouth drawn tight against the rage he was feeling until it was just a thin, hard line.

'Yes, doctor's orders!' he flung at her furiously, emotion heightening his accent dramatically. 'But I am no man's—or woman's—yes-man; no one's "parrot"! In this case I happen to believe that the cautious Dr Greene's policy is exactly right.'

'Y-you do?'

Another of those swift, sharp inclinations of his head to one side confirmed his words.

'I believe that it will be better for you to wait and see. To let time heal your mind and bring your memories back to you. I am convinced that it cannot be done quickly—nor should it be. You will remember when you are ready, not before! Why else do you think you are here?'

There was no way that Serena could answer that without

driving him into even greater fury. But even as she bit her lip against the impulsive words some change in her expression, a look in her eyes, had betrayed her, and she heard Rafael's breath hiss in through his teeth as he fought to control his own feelings.

'*Madre de Dios*, Serena! Why the devil are you so convinced that my reasons for having you here are evil? That they are motivated by—'

'Because otherwise it doesn't make sense!' Serena broke in on him desperately. 'Because people just don't do what you've done! They don't just pick up strange women off the streets and take them home with them, offer them food and lodging, a place to stay, unless…unless…'

'Unless,' Rafael repeated in a voice that had softened, deepened, become dangerously gentle. 'So now we are getting to it. Unless what, *mi belleza*? Precisely what ulterior motives do you believe are in my mind? Do you think that I have plans to hold you captive—sell you to the white slave trade?'

'Oh, now you're being ridiculous! Nothing like that ever crossed my mind.'

Though perhaps it should have done. She had taken Rafael's offer very much on trust, but really she knew nothing about him. The bang on the head she'd received really had addled her brain to make her agree to walking in blind like this.

'I was thinking more of the harm I could do—the problems I could cause because I don't know what happened. You've already brought up the problem with the driver and his family. If I hadn't known that I could have blundered in with both feet, hurting people without meaning to.'

Her words were greeted by a long, thoughtful silence. A silence in which her heart thudded heavily and uneasily, reacting fearfully to the slow, assessing scrutiny to which he subjected her. She felt like some particularly nasty, slimy specimen, laid out on a laboratory slide preparatory to being examined more closely under a microscope.

'If that is truly what is troubling you,' Rafael said at last, 'then I can assure you it will never happen.'

'Oh, really?'

Fighting down the sensation of having been judged and found very much wanting, at least in this man's estimation, Serena lifted her chin defiantly and forced her brown eyes to meet his. She was determined not to let him see the discomfort that cool appraisal had inflicted on her, no matter how much she felt bruised and battered inside.

'And you can promise me that, can you?'

His sudden movement made her start uncertainly, taking an uneasy step backwards as he came towards her. One long, tanned hand came out to close around her wrist, effortlessly holding her prisoner without any evidence of exerting any degree of force.

'I can swear it on the Bible, if that will convince you,' he declared with a deadly softness that was somehow far more forceful than if he had shouted at the top of his voice. 'Or on my own good name, and that of my family.'

'Which I suspect means much more to you than any religious book,' Serena couldn't resist inserting. 'So that must mean that you really think you can deliver.'

'Oh, I can deliver, all right,' Rafael drawled. 'If you trust me, I can promise you that as long as you are in my home, under my protection, I will ensure that you do not hurt anyone, in any way, as a consequence of the things you do not remember. I will take it on myself to act as a mediator between you and the rest of the world, and if ever there comes a time when I cannot keep my promise then I will tell you everything I know and go—get out of your life and stay out of it for ever.'

'That's quite some promise...'

Serena's voice shook uncontrollably, betraying the effect

his words had had on her, the force with which his deep-voiced avowal had hit home.

'And you really believe you can do this?'

'I know I can.'

The hand that held her wrist prisoner was unclasped, extended towards her in the age-old gesture of sealing a bargain.

'Do we have an agreement, Señorita Martin?'

If you trust me. The words swung round and round in Serena's head. *If you trust me. Could* she trust him?

It was Rafael or no one. There was no one else in her life to whom she could turn. No one else she could ask for help, or who would share the burden of her amnesia with her. Without Rafael she was completely alone.

Swallowing down the deep sigh that almost escaped her, she forced herself to put her hand into his.

'We have an agreement, Señor Cordoba,' she told him, praying she sounded convincing.

But as Rafael's strong fingers closed over hers, she had to will herself not to let him feel the instinctive tremor that revealed the uncertainty and confusion that still plagued her.

Why had she done this? *What* had she done? she asked herself, suddenly a prey to the terrible feeling that she had put her whole future, her whole life, in Rafael's hands, without any proof that he was in any way on her side at all.

CHAPTER FIVE

'SERENA!'

The sound of her name, the knock at the door of her room startled Serena out of her reverie so abruptly that she had to struggle to collect her scattered thoughts, bringing them back to the present only with an effort.

'Serena? Are you in there?'

Rafael's voice, of course. No one else could put quite that note of command into a simple question, or imply an impatience so close to breaking through any restraint imposed on it just by the use of her name.

How she wished she could pretend that she hadn't heard. Either that, or just ignore him completely. She wanted time to be on her own. Time to enjoy the seclusion of this room, the privacy of her own thoughts.

She didn't want to have to come out and talk to anyone, least of all the man who had brought her here. The man who so disturbed and unsettled her that her stomach contracted nervously simply at the thought of him, her heart lurching into a rapid, uneven patter that made it difficult to breathe.

But of course that was impossible. Already another rap of hard knuckles on the door, a rattle of the handle, warned her that what little patience Rafael had left was already growing thin. If she didn't respond, she suspected that, knowing the door was locked, he was more than capable of putting one strong shoulder to the wood and breaking it open.

'Serena!'

'All right,' she called unwillingly, having to force her voice into a volume loud enough to reach through the thickness of the door. 'I'm coming.'

'What the devil kept you?'

Rafael launched onto the attack the moment the door was open, sweeping into the room with all the arrogance and sense of command of some long-ago emperor or high-ranking general. So much so that Serena fully expected to see some sort of entourage forming behind him, attendant on his every whim.

'Didn't you hear my knock?'

'Oh, I heard all right!' Serena retorted satirically. 'It would have been hard to miss it. In fact, I suspect that your nearest neighbours—where was it you said they lived, five miles away, across the fields?—couldn't have missed the way you were banging at the door. Quite frankly I'm surprised that you didn't wake Tonio, making all that row.'

'He's fast asleep. I checked on my way here.'

Rafael shrugged off her annoyance with a carelessness that simply irritated her further.

'And now that you are here?' she asked acidly. 'I presume that there is some reason behind this—this invasion?'

'Aren't you aware of the time?'

Shooting back one immaculate white shirt cuff, Rafael brandished his gleaming gold watch directly under her nose.

'Time?' Serena echoed, unable to grasp quite what he was implying.

Her attempts to gather her muddled thoughts were further sabotaged by the sensual overload she had been enduring since the moment of his arrival. Just the sight of his tall, powerful body in the crisp white shirt, black linen jacket and trousers that he had changed into at some point earlier that evening made her insides flutter in heightened awareness.

She didn't want to be aware of the way that the perfect fit of the jacket sheathed Rafael's broad shoulders and chest like a second skin, the fine material of the trousers enhancing the strength of those long legs, the narrow hips and waist, with a care that was positively sinful. But, having once looked in his direction, she found it impossible to drag her wanton eyes away again, no matter how hard she tried. He had obviously showered very recently, and the scent of soap clung to him, the black hair still slightly damp.

And the way he had shoved his hand and wrist just under her nose was positively the last straw. She was burningly aware of every fine pore of the smoothly tanned skin and the way it slid and tensed with each movement of his strong, square-tipped fingers. The faint dusting of fine black hairs on his wrist and further up his arm made her own hands itch to reach out and touch, smooth along them, feel their delicate crispness under her fingertips. And the warm scent of his skin, sensually musky and overlaid with the slight tang of some lemony cologne, assailed her nostrils in a heady mixture that made her senses reel.

'What time is it?' she managed huskily.

Her hazy response earned her a testy click of his tongue in impatient reproof.

'It's eight-fifteen. Dinner should have been served over ten minutes ago.'

Vaguely Serena remembered him saying some such thing. 'But I didn't think you meant that I should eat with you. I mean, do the servants usually...?'

'*Dios!* You are not a servant!'

'No? Then would you mind telling me exactly what I am?'

'You are a guest...'

'A guest? I thought I was employed to look after Tonio. And would you bang on a *guest's* door as you have just done? March into a guest's room, demanding their presence at your—'

'Serena,' Rafael explained with exaggerated patience, 'you are just out of hospital, barely recovered from a nasty accident. When you didn't turn up for the meal, naturally I was concerned. I thought perhaps you were overtired—unwell.'

The golden gaze seared over her, taking in the pallor of her cheeks, shocking in contrast to the rich colour of her hair, her wide dark eyes.

'You are very pale. Do you feel okay? No headache—double vision—sickness?'

'No... Rafael, I'm fine!' she insisted when he still looked doubtful. 'Really I am! I'm sorry if I worried you. It's just that there have been so many shocks, so much to adjust to. I needed to be by myself for a while. If you must know—I was trying to remember!'

That was how the time had slipped away from her, the evening gathering in while she had gone back and back over every last little detail that she could remember, hoping against hope that one of them would trigger the missing links inside her head.

'It will not help...'

'Oh, I know you think I'm just wasting my time, but I have to do something! I can't just sit here and wait for something that may never come back to me if I don't *try*! If it was your memory that was missing, your life that was on hold like this, then could you do nothing?'

For the space of a slow count to six he considered the question, golden eyes narrowed thoughtfully. Then slowly he shook his dark head.

'No,' he conceded. 'I would have to try. But you have spent too much time brooding on your own. Put it to one side for tonight. Take a shower, get changed—and come and eat.'

Get changed.

For the first time Serena took in the full significance of the fact that Rafael was no longer dressed in the casual shirt and jeans he had worn earlier that day.

'I didn't realise that you expected me to change for dinner—but you'll have to excuse me. I'm afraid I don't have anything suitable.'

Rafael muttered something harsh and irritable in Spanish before striding swiftly across the room to fling open the doors of the wardrobe.

'And what do you think all this is? The collection for the local jumble sale?'

Serena knew that her jaw had dropped slightly, her mouth falling open in shock, and hastily she adjusted her expression.

'I'd—I'd assumed that those belonged to someone else. Someone who'd had the room before me. Your—Tonio's mother...'

'If you mean Elena, I told you, she and I were never married. And she never came to England, never spent any time in this house.'

'Then...'

Realisation dawned with the force of a blow to her skull so that she shook her head slightly, trying to clear her thoughts.

'You don't mean...?'

'Ah, but I do,' Rafael returned softly, gleaming eyes studying her from behind luxuriant black lashes, watching every fleeting expression that crossed her face.

'They can't be for me?'

'Who else?'

'I... No!'

Once more she shook her head, this time in fierce rejection. 'No way! You can't! I won't accept them!'

'But I bought them for you.'

'Well, you can just take them back again! I presume you still have the receipts. Of course you have. You're a banker; you'll think of things like that. You'd never—'

'Are you saying you don't like them?' Rafael enquired silkily, cutting in to the flow of her indignant protest. 'Would you prefer something else?'

'Like? Of course I like them!'

If the truth were told, when she had first discovered the clothes in the wardrobe she had been entranced, enchanted. She had delighted in the beautiful colours, the fine fabrics, stylish designs. And deep down she had been frankly envious of the woman she had believed owned such gorgeous and obviously expensive garments. They were the sort of things she would never have been able to afford for herself.

And that was precisely why she felt so tangled up inside at the realisation that Rafael had gone out looking for them, chosen them, bought them and hung them up in the wardrobe just for her.

'Then what's the problem, *cariña*?'

Forcing herself to ignore the fact that she strongly suspected *cariña* must be some sort of endearment in Spanish that he couldn't possibly mean, Serena scowled at him furiously, directing her blazing glare straight into his coolly impassive face.

'The problem, Señor Cordoba, is you! You and the way you seem determined to move in on my life and take it over! Ever since I woke up in that hospital you've been hell-bent on running things the way *you* want them, without a thought for what *I* want!'

'You don't want clothes?' Rafael enquired satirically. 'You must be the only woman in the world who doesn't.'

'Of course I wan—need clothes!' Serena flung at him in exasperation, a totally feminine pang of regret for the beautiful dresses, the stylish separates she was turning down putting an added bite into her words. 'But not those ones! I have partial amnesia—that doesn't mean I've totally lost my mind! Nor does it mean I'm a complete invalid. Yes, I need clothes, but I'll get my own.'

'With what?' One arched black brow curved upwards in mocking query. 'I mean, exactly what are you going to use to purchase these so-necessary items?'

'I...'

Totally nonplussed, Serena floundered, hunting for a way to answer him.

'Well, I—I presume that, seeing as you're employing me to take care of Tonio, you'll naturally be paying me something for the job?'

'Naturally,' Rafael confirmed with a swift, suspiciously sweet smile.

'Then I'll use that to buy myself clothes.'

Rafael's smile grew wider, took on a slant of wicked humour.

'And, tell me, what did you plan to wear in the meantime? Because no matter how much the idea of seeing you wandering about the house stark naked might appeal to me personally, I rather suspect that you would find such a situation a trifle...'

He paused, making a pretence of hunting for exactly the right word, which Serena had a pretty good idea was already firmly on the end of his taunting tongue.

'...impractical, shall we say?'

Not condescending to honour his mocking question with an answer, Serena tossed her head angrily, sending the coppery silk of her hair flying, her chin coming up as she faced him defiantly.

'I do have *some* clothes!' she reminded him tartly, praying that he wouldn't be able to look deep into her eyes and read the truth of her thoughts there. That comment about seeing her wandering around the house stark naked had been far too suggestive for comfort, and the sort of images it had sparked off in her wanton thoughts were provocative in the extreme.

She could feel a wave of hot colour flooding her cheeks as her mind threw up the fantasy of Rafael too wandering round the house stark naked, his gloriously toned body openly on display, the bronze velvet of his skin hers to touch and caress, the muscled arms and legs...

Ruthlessly she dragged her mind back from the erotic path it was intent on following and forced it on to the present.

'I have the basic minimum.'

'Which I provided for you,' Rafael reminded her, his tone pure honey.

'Which you provided for me,' Serena agreed between gritted teeth. 'But I'll pay you back! You know I will!'

'I don't want repayment,' Rafael said with a shrug. 'They were meant as a gift—as are these.'

His expansive gesture took in the multicoloured array hanging in the wardrobe.

'What I don't see is why these clothes are any different from the ones you accepted so readily before.'

'I had no choice in that—I was desperate.'

And, while she might be able to earn enough to repay Rafael for the cost of the couple of simple outfits he had provided for her to wear in the hospital, she had no chance at all of doing so for the large collection of items in the wardrobe. Every style, every fabric shrieked designer elegance—and designer expense.

She had no idea how much Rafael intended to pay her for her duties as a nanny, but she was pretty sure it wouldn't come anywhere near the small fortune that the clothes must have cost him.

'I have a choice now…'

'So you do,' Rafael inserted silkily, the softness of his voice making her instantly forget just what she had been about to say. 'You can choose to make me happy or to disappoint me bitterly.'

He actually looked as if he meant it. The golden eyes had darkened to the colour of a rich sherry, looking shadowed and opaque, the wide, sensual mouth turning down at the corners, confounding her completely.

'Disappoint you? I don't understand.'

'When I bought these clothes…'

Once more a bronzed hand swept along the rack of clothing, the gesture seeming to imply that the expensive garments were worth nothing, mere trifles to someone of his wealth and status.

'I bought them for one woman, and one woman only.'

'Me?' It was a breathless whisper, barely a sound, but Rafael caught it and nodded his dark head in response.

'You,' he confirmed, his voice deep and huskily enticing.

'I considered each one so carefully, tried to imagine what you would look like in it. In my mind I pictured how the colour would look against your hair…'

Long fingers reached out, brushed her hair, slid downwards over the gleaming strands.

'Your skin…'

That featherlight touch moved lower, caressed the soft skin of her cheek, traced the fine line of her jaw. Serena found that she had frozen into stillness, her throat drying, her heart barely beating. She was held transfixed, mesmerised by the enticing spell his whispered words were weaving around her.

'I chose things to enhance your eyes…'

This time it was his mouth that came close, brushing a butterfly kiss over each eyelid, closing them softly before drifting away again.

'Your neck…these delicate shoulders…'

As the warmth of Rafael's hands shaped the areas he named Serena had to fight to open her eyes. When her heavy lids finally struggled open it was to find that his strongly carved face was so close, only inches away from her own, his brilliant eyes burning down into her clouded, hazy brown ones.

'Raf…' She tried to form his name but he silenced her easily with a gentle fingertip laid across her mouth.

'All I could think of was your beauty, and the glory of your body, the curves of your breasts and hips, those long, slender legs. I wanted to see it dressed in the sort of clothing such loveliness deserves. I wanted nothing but the very best because you need the best, *mi belleza*. Only that and nothing more will do.'

'Rafael…' Serena tried again, her voice croaking as if she hadn't used it for years.

'Hush,' he soothed, the warm breath of his whisper stirring the soft hair at the nape of her neck. 'Don't talk—don't say anything. We both know what's going on here. What's really being said behind the careful, polite conversations.'

Serena's mind hazed; she couldn't speak, couldn't think.
There was nothing in her world but this man and the strength
of his arms as they held her, the warm scent of his skin in
her nostrils. She wanted to let that scent soak into her own
body, absorb it, absorb him completely. She needed to give
herself up to him, drown in the sensuality of his darkened
eyes, lose herself totally in him.

'And so, tonight, I know that you won't want to disappoint
me. That you won't want me to believe I bought these clothes
for all the wrong reasons.'

One hand slipped in at the scooped neckline of her blouse,
caressing the soft skin, drawing a moan of pleasure from her
lips. For a brief, telling second, the strong fingers rested
lightly on the spot at the base of her throat where the racing
pulse betrayed her inner excitement, and a slow, satisfied
smile curled the corners of his sensual mouth. His voice was
a rich purr of triumph when he spoke again.

'I want you to take those clothes, *mi* Serena, accept them
as a gift from me. Take them and wear them—wear them
tonight to please me. Can you do that, *cariña*?'

'Yes…' It was just a whisper, a sound that he had to bend
his dark head to hear. 'Yes, I can do that.'

She would do anything for him. Anything at all. If he
would only hold her, enclose her in his arms as he had just
done, keep her safe against the strength of his body. Her
pulse was a heavy, indolent throb in her veins, as if her blood
had thickened in the heat of the need that softened her bones,
made her whole body pliant against the iron-hard support of
his.

Against her hip she feel the heated evidence of the arousal
Rafael too was feeling, the proof of the fact that she was not
alone in the darkly sensual mood that had reached out to
enclose her, dragging her down until she was drowning in it.
The need, the ache that uncoiled, slow and sensuous, deep
in the most feminine part of her body, was shared, mutual,
impossible to resist.

In the grip of its voluptuous spell, she could only act as need directed, lifting her head blindly, offering her mouth for his kiss.

And was shocked into startled awakening as Rafael simply brushed her mouth with his, his caress almost brusque in its fleeting brevity, before he was withdrawing from her, putting her at arm's length, distancing himself physically as well as mentally.

'Then let's have no more argument, *belleza*. Our meal is waiting. If we delay any longer it will spoil.'

Briefly he glanced at his watch again, frowning faintly at what he saw.

'I will go downstairs and pour you a drink. You have— say, ten minutes to change. Make yourself beautiful, and join me. Can you manage that?'

Stunned by the abruptness of his withdrawal, her body aching at the loss of his so close to hers, Serena couldn't find her voice to answer him. She could only nod numbly, unable to keep up with the swift, unexpected changes of his mood.

Just a moment before she had been so sure that all he wanted was to kiss her, caress her. If he had lifted her in his arms and carried her to the bed she would have made no protest. She would have gone with him willingly, happily, a slave to the desire his touch sparked off along every cell in her body. Even now, her skin still tingled where he had touched her, her awakened nerves protesting at the sudden abandonment of the pleasure they had anticipated with such delight.

But in the space of a heartbeat Rafael had withdrawn completely, his tone becoming brisk and businesslike, all trace of the sinfully confident lover evaporating like the mist before sun.

'Ten minutes, then,' he said crisply. 'I will wait for you downstairs.'

And in the moment that he spoke Serena looked into his

tanned face and saw the change in his eyes and knew that she had been wrong. The lover hadn't gone, driven away by Rafael's change of mood. He was still there in the lustrous golden depths of those mesmerising eyes, burning incandescently behind the thick fringe of impossibly long lashes. But for his own reasons, for some purpose she couldn't begin to guess at, Rafael had applied the brakes hard, reining in the hunger she had sensed in him so potently, ruthlessly bringing it under an almost brutal control.

'Ten minutes…' she managed, her voice shaking as much in disappointment as uncertainty and confusion.

Her reward was a swift, predatory smile, and with a sudden movement Rafael reached out, touching her cheek and cupping its softness in the warmth of his palm for a brief, heart stopping moment.

'I'll be waiting,' he promised in a voice whose husky softness could not conceal the raw note of need that threaded through it jaggedly, darkening and disturbing it in the same way that cruel, dangerous rocks lurk unobserved at the bottom of the smoothest sea.

And in that moment the truth hit home with a near physical impact that parted her lips on a gasp of shocked realisation. She knew what Rafael was doing, just what was in his mind.

In the moment that he had taken her into his arms he had asked her a silent, subtle question. And in the same manner her body's instinctive reaction, her mindless response to his touch, had given him the answer he had wanted.

It had been male to female communication in its most basic, most primal form, without words, almost at a telepathic level. And yet everything that had to be said had been conveyed, like an electrical current passing between them. And now they could step back a moment and wait.

She didn't know why Rafael had changed his mind about waiting until her memory returned before taking their relationship a stage further. Didn't know and didn't care. What was coming was inevitable, and because of that there was no need to rush. They could slow the pace a little, enjoy the dalliance, the anticipation that would make the pleasure of their coming together all the greater when it finally arrived.

And, realising that, she could smile and nod, and murmur, 'I won't keep you long,' knowing he would see what was behind her answer and that it would add to his pleasure to see just how they were attuned to each other, exactly on the same wavelength.

The warmth of Rafael's smile washed over her, making her toes curl on the rich wool carpet, clenching on the soft turquoise pile. She could actually enjoy the sting of deprivation that twisted at her senses now that she knew it was only temporary. She could nurture it and let it grow, like a slow-burning fuse heading steadily, inexorably, towards a keg of gunpowder. The resulting explosion would be so much greater, so much more violent as a result.

'See you downstairs,' he said, lifting his hand in a small, casual wave.

'It won't be for long,' Serena returned, knowing she didn't just mean the length of time between now and their meal.

In the doorway Rafael paused, turning briefly so that his burning eyes met hers.

'Wear the bronze, Serena,' he ordered firmly. 'I've a fancy to see you in the bronze.'

The bronze, Serena repeated, heading for the wardrobe as soon as she was alone. If the bronze was what he fancied, then the bronze was what he'd get.

Her smile was warm, secretive, pure female, as she held the soft silk of the dress Rafael had chosen against her body and swayed in a sensual little dance before the mirror.

He had chosen well. She could already imagine what the sleeveless dress with its vee neckline and slim, pencil skirt would look like on her slender body.

Oh, yes, the bronze would be perfect. And so would be the evening ahead of her. The evening that she knew would end with Rafael and herself becoming lovers for the very first time.

CHAPTER SIX

'WOULD you like more coffee?'

The meal was over, the plates pushed to one side, and Serena and Rafael lingered over coffee and mints, the candles that had lit the table burning down low in their holders.

'Not for me, thanks.'

Serena shook her head with a smile.

'Any more and I'll not sleep at all tonight.'

She didn't need the caffeine anyway. She already felt totally wired on enjoyment, high on the atmosphere alone.

'We can't have that.'

Rafael's slow smile made her feel as if she was melting inside, her stomach twisting as she looked into the darkness of his eyes.

'Tonio always wakes around six o' clock in the morning. You'll need some rest if you're to be able to cope with him for a full day. That reminds me...'

Draining what was left of his wine, he pushed back his chair and stood up.

'I'd better go and check on him, make sure he's still asleep. Won't be a moment.'

'Take as long as you like,' Serena assured him. 'I'll be fine here.'

She could do with a few minutes to herself, she reflected as Rafael left the room. A short time to draw breath, try to calm the pounding race of her heart that had been turning somersaults inside her chest with every smile Rafael had flashed in her direction, every caressing glance of those deep golden eyes.

The hunger, the need she had seen in him earlier were still there and he had made no pretence at hiding them. As a

70

result, her nerves had been stretched tight with excitement and anticipation all evening. If she continued at this pitch she would snap apart with tension.

Her skin felt hypersensitive, tantalised by every brush of her hair over her shoulders. The slide of the bronze silk dress over her body was a tinglingly sensual sensation that made her shiver in pure delight. She could almost imagine that the feelings were created by the touch of Rafael's hands, the caress of his lips, and heat pooled at the most intimate centre of her body in anticipation of what was yet to come.

'You'll need some rest, Rafael had said, she recalled as she blew out what remained of the candles and then, with her half-empty wine glass in her hand, got to her feet and wandered out of the elegant dining room. The night was warm and she needed some air and so she headed for the huge, Victorian-style conservatory with its black and white tiled floor. But she knew that 'rest' was the exact opposite of what he had planned for the rest of the night.

When he came back from checking on Tonio, she felt sure that Rafael would take her in his arms. He would hold her close and the reality of his kisses would replace the fantasies she had allowed herself to indulge in, the anticipation that had kept her on tenterhooks throughout the long, lingering meal.

'We both know what's going on here.' She repeated his words to her earlier, speaking them out loud, unable to hold back a bubbling laugh of excitement. 'Oh, yes, we know— we know all right!'

Needing to express the thrill that shivered through her in some form of physical action, she spun round on her heels, round and round again, faster and faster, until at last she lost her balance and stumbled. With a cry of shock she flung out a hand, catching hold of a small pine coffee table to support herself and sending the pile of magazines on the top of it flying.

'Oh, no!'

Putting down her glass hastily, she knelt on the floor, picking up the scattered items, bundling them back together. But as she lifted one glossy magazine she paused abruptly, staring down in stunned confusion at the photograph that lay beneath it.

'What...?'

Slowly she reached out to pick it up, a cold, creeping sensation like the tread of tiny icy footprints sliding down her spine as she met the eyes of the woman in the photograph. Wide, beautiful, almond-shaped eyes, dark, shining eyes above stunningly beautiful cheekbones, a full, smiling mouth. The woman had long, glossy black hair, an aristocratic bone structure and something indefinable about her that declared eloquently that there was no way she could be anything but Spanish.

'This must be...'

'Elena,' a low, harsh-toned voice finished from behind her, bringing her to her feet in a rush and swinging her round to stare at the man who had come in, soft-footed as a cat, unnoticed behind her.

Elena. Tonio's mother.

Serena's eyes dropped to the photograph again, looking for traces of Rafael's son in the woman's face. They weren't easy to find. So far the little boy was pure Cordoba, taking after his father's side of the family.

'She's—she's very beautiful.'

It was an effort to speak. In the moment that she had first seen the photograph her heart had clenched painfully, fighting against the knowledge that if Rafael still had this woman's picture in his home, perhaps his relationship with Elena was not as dead as she had anticipated.

Tonio's mother and I are not, as you so tactfully put it, 'together'. That was all he had said. Those few curt words had given no indication as to how he felt about the situation, whether he had been happy to let her go or still carried a torch for her deep in his heart.

'*Was* very beautiful,' Rafael corrected harshly, the raw emphasis giving the first word a terrible, shocking finality.

'Was...?' Serena couldn't believe what she had heard. 'Rafael...'

With the autocratic gesture that was fast becoming very familiar to her Rafael held out his hand for the photograph, no words needing to be spoken. He knew very well that she would interpret his wishes without them. Which, of course, she did, handing the picture to him as she got slowly to her feet.

'What happened?' she managed shakily as he looked down at the picture in sombre silence, eyes hooded, hiding all emotion from her.

'She died,' Rafael said at last, expelling the words on a raw, broken sigh. 'Breast cancer.'

'But she was so young!' The horror Serena felt rang in her voice. She couldn't bear to think of someone so obviously vibrant and alive, someone clearly very close to her own age, no longer even existing.

'Young—and pregnant,' Rafael confirmed heavily. 'She was told she could have treatment, but it would harm the baby. She wouldn't even consider that prospect, so she refused. That decision killed her.'

'Oh, my God! Rafael, I—'

'No...'

With a violent movement he twisted away from the hand that reached for him, the arms that wanted to enfold him.

'I do not want your comfort, your tears, Serena. Spare me that at least.'

'Spare you?'

She couldn't understand the reasons behind his rejection, only knew that it clawed savagely at her heart, leaving it raw and wounded.

'And I—I'm not crying!'

'No?'

On a growl of exasperation he strode forward, catching

hold of her arms, imprisoning her and swinging her round to face him. One hand came up to her face, the pad of the thumb stroking under her left eye. To Serena's consternation it came away with a single teardrop glistening on its tip. A tear she had not even been aware of having shed.

'Then what is this, *mi belleza?*'

'I—I...'

Puzzled and hurt by his reaction, she found herself wanting to lash out, to wipe the strangely accusing expression from that sculpted face with words if not with the flat of her hand. The contrast between the softly tingling anticipation of just moments before and this unexpected and, in her mind, inexplicable confrontation was jarring and bewildering.

'So I'm crying!' she flung at him, her bright head going back, eyes flashing. 'And what's wrong with that? That story—about Elena—it's tragic, desperately sad. Who wouldn't want to weep when they heard it? Anyone would—'

'Anyone!' Rafael broke in savagely. 'Anyone, perhaps— but not you. Not you, *belleza*. Why should you weep over the story of a woman you have never met, never seen except in that photograph? Why should the ready tears spring to your eyes now when they—*Dios!*'

He snapped the words off viciously, releasing her arm with an eloquent gesture of distaste and swinging away from her to stare broodingly out of the window, shoulders hunched, hands pushed deep into his trouser pockets.

Serena could only stare at the stiff, straight line of his back, seeing rejection stamped into every inch, every taut muscle. It was almost as if, in the time that he had been out of the room, Rafael had been transformed into someone else entirely.

She couldn't believe that he was the same man who had sat opposite her all evening, who had entertained her with sparkling, witty conversation. The same Rafael who had displayed the sort of natural, effortless charm that would have enticed all the birds out of the trees, never mind one foolish woman whose too-vulnerable heart was already halfway to falling in love with him.

There, she'd admitted it to herself. The feelings she had for Rafael went further and deeper than just the powerful attraction she had felt from the first. She came alive in his presence, every sense on red alert. When she was with him every experience was intensified, ever colour brighter, every scent sweeter, every sound sharper.

But was that *love*? Was it possible to love someone you knew so little about? Someone you had met only a few days—barely a week—ago? No, she was deluding herself, being fanciful. The reality was that because of her loss of memory Rafael was in many ways the only person she really knew right now. That and her present vulnerable state of mind had made her respond to him with her heart rather than her head.

'Rafael...' she said hesitantly, needing to break through the barriers he had suddenly flung up around himself. 'I don't understand. Do you—do you want to talk about it?'

That brought him whirling round, and the sight of his face had her taking a couple of involuntary steps backwards in shock. His skin was pale and drawn tight over the strong bone structure, his jaw set. His eyes were dark and shadowed, marks like bruises showing underneath them. And the hunger that had burned in them, sparking the fizzing excitement deep in her own heart, seemed to have been totally extinguished, blotted out like the sun going behind a cloud.

'No, Serena, I do not want to talk about it! I do not want to talk about Elena, or her beauty, or the days I spent with her—the night I got her pregnant with my child.'

'I didn't mean that!' Serena protested, knowing that, feeling as she did now, that was the last thing she wanted to listen to anyway.

She couldn't bear to hear how he had adored the other woman, how he had spent long, long nights with her, making wild, passionate love. The love that had created the beautiful little boy now sleeping soundly upstairs.

'And I do not want to talk about her too-brief life and the tragic way it was cut short. That is not what I want from you!'

'This is not what you want,' Serena echoed bitterly, no longer caring if her voice betrayed the pain and turmoil twisting inside her. 'That is not what you want. You make it so very obvious just what I'm doing wrong, but you do nothing at all to let me know what is right. Nothing to tell me what you *do* want from me!'

The silence that followed her outburst was so profound, so taut, that it tugged hard on her already overstretched nerves, pulling them out to near snapping point. Say something! she wanted to cry. Say anything, anything at all, even if it's only go to hell!

But at the same time she didn't want him to speak. Deep inside she was terrified that he would turn on her, tell her to go, dismiss her from his life without a second thought. And she didn't know how she would cope with that. He had become so important to her so quickly that she couldn't bear even to contemplate the emptiness, the desolation of her soul that would result if he turned away from her now.

But then at last Rafael drew in a long, ragged breath, expelling it again on a heavy sigh as he raked both hands through his thick black hair, shaking his head faintly.

'Oh, Serena,' he said, his voice low and strangely hoarse. 'Do you even have to ask? I thought it was transparently obvious what I want from you.'

How could she ever have thought that the hunger had gone from his eyes? It was still there, still blazing every bit as incandescently as before, turning his eyes into dangerous flames of desire, giving them the fierce burn of lasers as they seemed to scorch over her skin.

'You know what I want—what I've always wanted. You don't need to be told—at least not in words. Because it's what you want too. I've known that from the first. I can read it in your eyes when you look at me, hear it in your voice when you speak.'

Once again a powerful bronzed hand was lifted in that haughty gesture that was so typically Rafael. A long finger curved, arrogantly beckoning her to come to him, and she found that she had actually moved, lifting one foot in order to obey without question, when a new, stronger reason asserted itself, stilling her swiftly.

'I don't know what you mean.'

Since the moment that Rafael had come back into the room he had taken her on such a roller-coaster ride of emotions, subjected her to so many switches of mood, so many vagaries of feeling, that she was quite exhausted from trying to keep up. He had turned on her in anger, rejected her so brutally that she could still feel the ache his words had inflicted deep inside. And now he wanted—expected—her to go to him as soon as he so much as lifted a little finger in summons.

Well, he was going to have to work a little harder than that.

'What exactly are you talking about?'

Oh, he hadn't liked that—not one little bit. Evidently the great Rafael Cordoba was accustomed to having his women—and very probably many men too—jump to attention as soon as he clicked his fingers. The swift, dark frown that drew his arched brows together warned of trouble if she pushed him further.

'Don't play games, Serena!' he snapped coldly. 'It doesn't suit you.'

'What games?' Serena matched his tone ice for ice. 'I'm deadly serious. From the moment I woke up in that hospital bed I've known only too well that you have some sort of hidden agenda for me. Some plan that you're not prepared to let me in on.'

Rafael's sigh was a masterpiece of resigned exasperation.

'This is not relevant…'

'Not to you perhaps, but it's relevant to *me*! I want to know what gave you the right—'

'You gave me the right,' Rafael inserted with icy calm, stopping her dead.

'I did? How—when?'

'In the moment that you accepted the clothes I bought you, the hospital room I paid for. When you agreed to come here with me.'

'I...'

Try as she might, she couldn't get the protest to form. This was a new Rafael. Or rather not new, but the first one she had ever seen, the cold-eyed predator who had been in her hospital room when she had first awakened. The man whose watchful gaze and tautly held body made her think of a skilled hunter just waiting for the right moment at which to pounce. This was the Rafael who had been carefully hidden for so long that she had almost forgotten his existence. But now she was forced to face the fact that this one was the real one.

'But really, we both know it started before that,' Rafael continued with malign softness. 'It was there in that first moment. In the second that you opened your eyes and looked at me...'

'No...' Desperately she shook her head, refusing to let his words really penetrate her mind, take root.

'Yes,' he corrected, so smoothly that the word was almost a caress in itself. 'And to deny it is to deny part of yourself. You forget that I have held you, kissed you. I have felt your response, a response that I know you can neither hide nor fake. So why don't we stop playing games, hmm?'

'I'm playing at nothing!' Serena retorted. 'On the contrary, I'm deadly serious!'

When had he moved? She would have sworn that she hadn't seen him take a single step and yet suddenly he was closer, worryingly, unnervingly so.

He was near enough for her to see the burn of something

dangerous in his eyes, the rigid control that tightened his jaw, clamped his mouth into a cruel line. Every trace of the sexual electricity that had emanated from him only moments earlier was gone, erased as if by the flick of a switch, and all that was left was a cold aura of something ominous and threatening.

'And so am I.'

His tone was definitely menacing now.

'I have never been more serious in my life. That is why I am losing patience with your childish prevaricating, the way you blow hot and cold almost as often as you breathe.'

'*I* blow hot and cold? And what about you? In the hospital, it was "Not ever, if I am wise"; now—'

'Now I am admitting that when I am with you any wisdom I possess evaporates like a mist before the sun. I cannot fight it any longer. What there is between us is meant to be, and the sooner you accept that, the easier it will be.'

'Easy!' Serena echoed. 'Easier for you or for me?'

Rafael's smile was slow and wickedly confident, matching the gleam in his dark eyes.

'For *both* of us, *mi amor.*'

Somehow he had come close enough to be able to reach out and touch her, his index finger moving to trace a gentle line down her cheek in a gesture that was both caress and threat in one.

'There is no need for all this, believe me. Playing hard to get will not make me want you more.'

Ignoring her gasp of shocked protest, he continued with another of those ominous smiles.

'I have no restraint where you are concerned—none at all. Any control I had vanished in the moment that I saw you lying in that hospital bed, and it has only been out of consideration for your delicate state of health that I have held back. But not any more.'

'And am I supposed to be *grateful* for that? For the fact

that you allowed me time to recover before you made your intentions plain?'

What was she doing? Only a short time before she had been fizzing with excitement, eagerly anticipating being taken to this man's bed, becoming his lover. And yet now she was hell-bent on pushing him away, creating as much distance as was possible between them and making him so angry in the process that she was in danger of having him reject her completely.

But the man she had wanted so badly had been someone else, not this cruel-faced predator whose eyes promised retribution if she didn't fall in with his plans without a word of protest.

'And if that was *restraint*, or *consideration* then, believe me, I've seen charging bulls that could show you a thing or two about both of those traits and then some!'

'And I know of a hyena that could be put to shame by having its shriek compared with yours!' Rafael returned with grim humour. 'You would argue the hind leg off a donkey. It seems that the only way to shut you up is to do this...'

Before she could even register the way his thoughts were heading she was grabbed by iron-hard hands, hauled up against the solid wall of his chest and kissed with ruthless, cold-blooded efficiency.

And the appalling thing was that even as she recognised that this kiss was a form of control, of punishment, with no trace of real affection or passion in it, it still had the same effect on her as that other, less brutal assault on her senses in her hospital room the day before. It heated her blood, made her heart pound, her head swim, her thoughts blurring in the whirlwind of sensation.

She felt his hands in her hair, raking through the soft strands then linking together at the nape of her neck, crushing her close, keeping her mouth against his, holding her captive so that she could not break free if she tried to.

But Serena was incapable of even summoning up the will

to try. Her knees threatened to buckle, unable to support her, and she sagged against Rafael, thankful that his strength was there to hold her up.

'You go up in flames when I touch you,' he hissed in her ear, the throatily triumphant note barely audible above the pounding of her heart. 'I like that—more than like it! It shows that you and I are one, in this at least. You make me ache like no woman ever has before and in return I will make you feel that no other man has ever touched you.'

And there it was. There, in one simple phrase—or rather not simple, but inexpressibly complicated and responsible for so much emotional turmoil that her mind practically blew a fuse just thinking of it—was the real crux of the matter.

With a choking cry Serena wrenched her mouth away from his, the force of her reaction sending her spinning across the room, putting out her arms hastily to stop herself from slamming into the wall.

'But don't you see?' she flung at him, huge brown eyes pleading with him for understanding, for some tiny ray of sensitivity to break through the cold, hard mask that was his expression. 'That's just the problem!'

'What problem, exactly?'

If she had hoped for sympathy then her wish was agonisingly far from being answered. Instead, the slash of his voice, the golden ice of his eyes stripped away what little was left of her self-assurance so that she had to put her shaking palms against the wall at her back in order to keep herself upright.

'I don't know!' she cried in a voice that soared upwards in an uneven wail, quavered and then broke into a muddle of sounds and sighs that bore no relation to the true content of her feelings. Rafael had to concentrate hard even to understand the drift of her words. 'I don't know if this has happened before—if any man has touched me before—has...has...'

'Do you think I care?'

She expected, and got, the imperious gesture that discarded her fears without a second thought.

'Do you think the past matters? What concerns me is here and now, in this room at this moment. All I care about is what there is between you and me, and the blazing sexual high we create between us.'

Serena's fingers clenched hard, digging into the wall, as if by doing so she could draw on some of its hard strength, its inanimate absence of feeling to sustain her through this confrontation.

'It's not enough!'

'It is for me. It's all I want, all I care about...'

'And you would use me for that...that temporary satisfaction...'

'We would use each other,' Rafael corrected almost gently. 'And there is no need for it to be as temporary as you fear. On the contrary, *mi corazón*, I doubt if a few days, a few weeks, will be enough to ease the craving that you have woken in me. And I would not just take.'

She'd touched him on his macho pride there, Serena reflected bitterly. He'd interpreted her words as a reflection on his expertise as a lover, and was determined to refute the accusation he believed she had thrown at him.

'I could make it so very good for you. I would give you every pleasure you have ever dreamed of.'

And some she had never even begun to imagine. She knew that with him her nights could be glorious, at first spent in the delirium of passion that this man could create in her, and then falling deeply asleep in his arms. But inevitably the morning would come, and with it the cold light of day. She would have to wake and look at herself in the mirror, and when she did so would she like what she saw?

'Serena...'

His voice had dropped an octave, softening, becoming the sort of soothing, cajoling whisper that one might use to quieten a nervous, highly-strung thoroughbred. And as he spoke he came towards her, his footsteps silent on the thick carpet, slowly and inexorably closing in on her again.

'Don't fight me on this, *belleza*. Don't resist what you know is inevitable. Like a butterfly beating its wings against a window pane, you will only hurt yourself if you struggle against something you cannot vanquish.'

Someone had nailed her feet to the floor. She couldn't move, her rebellious body refusing to even try, no matter how her mind screamed at it to do so. She couldn't even twist her head away when he reached out and trailed the backs of his knuckles softly down her cheek, making her shiver in uncontrollable response.

'And I do not want you to hurt—I want you to feel, to enjoy. I want you to know what you do to me...'

Catching hold of one of the slender hands still splayed out against the wall, he pulled her closer, unashamedly pressing her trembling fingers against the heated hardness that was the force of his desire for her. Golden eyes blazed down into hers, drying her throat, scrambling what was left of her ability to think.

'You asked what I want from you, well, I will tell you. I want a present. I want some pleasure, some happiness right here and now. Elena, and the tragedy of her short life, is in the past, but I am still very much alive. What I want from you, I want today. Today, and for however long this thing between us lasts.'

This thing! That got through. It was like a cruel knife twisting in her heart, making her want to scream against the pain.

Elena was the past; she, it seemed, was to be his present. And the future? Clearly there was to be no place for her in whatever hereafter Rafael envisaged for himself.

'"Today, and for however long this thing between us lasts!"' She spat his own words back at him, lacing them with all the venom she could drag up from her desolated soul. 'And how long would that be, precisely? A month? Two if I'm lucky?'

The careless shrug of those broad shoulders under the immaculately tailored jacket only incensed her further. A red haze floated before her eyes, destroying her vision. And just as well. If she had had to look into his stunning face it would have destroyed her, turning the words to ashes in her mouth.

'To a man who can't even mourn his dead love properly, I must suppose that a paltry six weeks would seem like a lifetime.'

'*Cristo!*' Rafael exploded, a stream of violent, dark-toned Spanish escaping him as he lost his grip on his temper once and for all. 'How dare you, you little witch? How dare *you*, of all people, accuse me of a lack of love, of—'

'Oh, *I* don't accuse you, Rafael! I don't need to.'

Serena had the bit well and truly between her teeth now, and she couldn't have caught herself up if she had tried. The words spilled out of her, fast and furious, tumbling over themselves in her need to fling them into his face.

'The evidence is all too clear anyway. You stand accused, convicted and condemned by your own words, your own actions! You told me yourself that Tonio isn't even three months old yet! That being the case, then even if your beautiful Elena died in the moment of his birth she hasn't been gone for twelve whole weeks! Not even ninety days, you cold-hearted, stinking louse! You offer me an affair for as long as it lasts, but the truth is…'

To her horror she felt the hot sting of tears in her eyes, threatening to spill over and cascade down her cheeks, betraying the fact that her anger hid another, deeper, and much more hazardous emotion. One that, if he should guess at it, would leave her hopelessly vulnerable to him, defenceless against the determined sexual campaign he was waging against her.

'The truth—' she tried again, but was interrupted by his savage curse.

'The truth!' Rafael repeated in a voice that froze all the blood in her veins, extinguishing the liberating anger in a second as effectively as if he had doused her with icy water. '*La verdad*, if you really knew it, my dear Serena, is nothing at all like the picture you have painted. But if you are so insistent upon it, then I shall tell you *the truth*. Because you see—'

But he got no further. Just as he drew breath to continue he was interrupted by a small whimpering sound from behind him.

'What?'

Rafael's dark head snapped round in confusion as, frowning, he hunted for the source of the sound.

Serena was there before him. Every instinct suddenly on red alert, she recognised the cry of distress relayed to them by the baby monitor in every room just before it rose from a sob into an agonising crescendo of a wail.

'Tonio!' she shouted, already heading for the door. 'It's Tonio and he's really upset!'

The last words were torn from her as she reached the stairs, dashing up them as swiftly as she could, Rafael just a couple of steps behind her.

CHAPTER SEVEN

'DO YOU think we've finally won?' Serena asked, keeping her voice to a soft whisper.

Rafael looked down at the small bundle of humanity in her arms, and smiled slightly wearily.

'We're getting there, I think. But I wouldn't bet a fortune on it. After all that that little villain has put us through to-night, I'll never be confident about saying he's asleep ever again.'

'He has certainly proved that there's nothing wrong with his lungs,' Serena admitted wryly. 'But I do believe that he's actually giving in now. A couple more minutes should do it.'

She kept her eyes fixed on the dark, downy top of Tonio's small head as she spoke, not yet ready to look the man opposite her straight in the face. He was too close, the mood too quietly intimate for her to be able to cope with meeting his eyes and reading what might be in them after their confrontation earlier that evening.

At the beginning it hadn't mattered. By the time they had reached Tonio's bedroom—Rafael, whose longer legs had enabled him to take the stairs two at a time, arriving a couple of seconds in front of her—Tonio had been screeching so loudly and had turned so red in the face that he had been their primary consideration. They had been able to think of nothing beyond calming him down, comforting him and returning him to the pale wooden cot in which he slept.

But Tonio had refused to be comforted. Even though the principal reason for his distress had been obvious from the moment they had run into his room, to find Conejo the small stuffed rabbit lying on the ground, simply returning his favourite toy had not pacified the little boy. In spite of his obvious tiredness, and the fact he had been held safely in Rafael's arms, he had twisted and turned, waving his arms frantically and kicking out with his legs, showing no sign of calming down.

'He's obviously hungry,' Rafael said at last. 'Can you hold him while I go downstairs and make up a bottle?'

'Are you sure about that?' Serena asked warily. 'I mean, of course I don't mind holding him, but don't you think he'd be happier with his daddy while I prepare the bottle?'

'And he's so happy with his *daddy* right now,' was Rafael's ironic comment as once more the baby stiffened and thrashed about in his arms. 'You might just have better luck. Besides, I know where everything is in the kitchen. You'd have to hunt around for what you wanted.'

'Okay, then...' Serena held out her arms. 'Come to me, you little monster.'

It seemed to her that Rafael hesitated for a telling second or two before he responded. That those tawny eyes were suddenly turned on her face in a swift flash of assessment so sharp, so intent that she felt it had actually scoured over her skin, leaving it raw and sensitive.

But just as she was about to protest, to ask if he didn't trust her with his precious son, the strangely watchful expression vanished and the still-wailing baby was deposited carefully into her arms.

'I'll take care of him, I promise,' she said sharply, not really understanding exactly why she had even spoken, only knowing that Rafael seemed to need the reassurance. 'I may not have much experience with little ones, but I'll do my best.'

'I'm sure you will.' Rafael's voice was surprisingly gruff. 'I'll only be downstairs.'

Still he seemed strangely reluctant to leave.

'We'll be fine,' Serena assured him. 'I'll give a shout if I need you.'

For a moment Rafael's hand rested against the baby's

cheek, and, as it had in the hospital, on the first day she had seen Tonio, the contrast between the man's strength, so carefully controlled into gentleness, and the baby's tiny size tore at Serena's heart. Blinking hard, she had to bite her lip against the tears that sprang hot and stinging into her eyes.

'Hush, *mi corazón*,' he whispered huskily. 'Don't distress yourself so.'

Tonio stilled for a moment, looking up at the dark, masculine face above his, his cries turning into a hiccuping sob as he drew an uneven breath. But just as Serena began to wonder if the tempest was finally over and they had reached a lull in the storm, his expression changed again and he launched into another angry yell.

'Okay, okay!' Rafael's tone was wry. 'So nothing but a bottle will pacify you. It's on its way!'

Left alone, listening to his hurried footsteps descending the stairs, Serena acted purely on instinct, cuddling the hot and bothered baby close to her and pacing slowly up and down the room. From somewhere at the back of her mind came a long ago memory of a song, an old-fashioned nursery rhyme that her mother had once sung to her, and automatically she began crooning it to the little boy.

'Sing a song of sixpence, a pocketful of rye, four-and-twenty blackbirds baked in a pie...'

It seemed to be working. Something seemed to be working anyway. Tonio's yells quietened, as if in curiosity at hearing the new and unfamiliar voice. He lay still, big eyes staring unblinkingly up at her.

'That's better, is it, sweetheart? What else do you like?'

Scrambling round in her memory, she dragged up another song and began on that, rocking Tonio in her arms as she did so, trying to keep her voice soft and soothing.

With another of those small, hiccuping little sounds, the baby actually started to relax. He stopped thrashing about with his arms and legs and as his shrieks eased his face started to resume its natural colour.

'Oh, now we're getting somewhere,' Serena encouraged him, feeling more confident as Tonio's tension eased. She didn't dare to stop moving, however, but continued to walk up and down the room, still singing softly.

The warm, soft weight of Tonio's body in her arms was a delight to her as she cuddled him close. His sweet, clean baby smell, with its mixture of talcum powder and the lotion Rafael had used, made her want to bury her face in his neck and inhale deeply.

Held tight against the warmth of her body, the baby sighed suddenly and then twisted in her arms, his little face turned against the bronze silk of her dress, nestling close, his mouth questing, nuzzling against her breast.

'Oh, darling! You *are* hungry. But I'm afraid there's nothing there for you.'

Her voice shook as something about the baby's vulnerability, his instinctive, trusting response, wrenched at her heart, love sharp as a pain welling up in a sudden powerful rush. She suddenly knew, with a conviction beyond all reason, that she would do anything, anything at all, to keep this child safe, protect him from any sort of harm.

'But don't worry. Daddy will bring the milk soon.'

Once more she began to pace the room, singing another nursery rhyme. She was so absorbed in what she was doing that she didn't hear Rafael's returning footsteps on the stairs or notice him coming into the room. It was only when she turned at the far side of the nursery, about to walk back the way she had come, that she became aware of him standing silently in the doorway, dark eyes fixed on her, just watching her.

'Oh, you startled me! I didn't hear you come in.'

'Obviously.'

There was a note in his voice she couldn't even begin to interpret, but his eyes were giving nothing away as he came into the room, his attention apparently switched to the child in her arms.

'You seem to have the magic touch.'

'I just sang to him—a lot of nonsense I remember from my own childhood.'

'Well, let's just hope that this...' he indicated the bottle of milk in his hand '...will just finish things off.'

He was close to her now, and automatically she moved to pass the baby over to him to be fed.

'No.'

The word rasped in his throat and he had to clear it briefly before he could continue.

'Better not to disturb him. You give him his bottle. Sit here...'

With his hand on her arm, he led her to the deep blue softly padded chair with a high back that stood against the wall by the window.

'Comfortable?'

Too many emotions tangled and knotted halfway up her throat to allow Serena to speak, and she could only nod silently, wide brown eyes locking with his deep golden ones as he looked down at her.

'Right, *gatito*...'

One-handed Rafael flipped the cap off the bottle and held it out.

'I think this is what you were demanding.'

Serena felt as if she was living through a dream, her actions seeming to be carried out in slow motion as she reached for the bottle, adjusted Tonio's position so that his head rested against her arm and placed the bottle against his lips. A snatch of delighted laughter escaped her as she saw the alacrity and enthusiasm with which his mouth opened and then closed around the teat, sucking enthusiastically.

'Look at him!' With a gentle finger she lightly touched one peach-soft cheek. 'Anyone would think he'd never been fed all day! He's a little glutton, isn't he? He...'

Her words trailed off, failing her completely as something about the silence of the man at her side penetrated her delight, making her glance round in sudden consternation. He was watching her again, those hawk's eyes fastened on her face, not Tonio's.

'What—what is it?'

Anxiety bubbled under the words, making her voice come and go unevenly.

'Am I doing something wrong?'

'You're doing fine,' he told her, his accent suddenly unexpectedly strongly marked. 'Tonio's perfectly relaxed. He's feeding well. What more could you want?'

That this could be real. That it could go on for ever. That Tonio could be ours—yours and mine—and we could care for him as real parents, not just nanny and employer.

She didn't know where the words had come from, couldn't even have said that she had formed them rationally. Instead, they seemed to have sprung from some deep, hidden part of her subconscious, from her heart, where they had been growing, unseen and unknown until this moment.

'Should I let him have it all?' she managed shakily, feeling the burning imprint of his watchful eyes on the soft exposed skin of her neck.

'If he wants it.' Rafael's voice was low. 'Then perhaps he'll let us have the rest of the night in peace.'

The rest of the night. The words held a significance that made her shiver involuntarily. In the switchback of moods and emotions that had assailed her ever since she had first set foot in this house, she had no idea what was coming next.

The truth, Rafael had said in the last moments downstairs before Tonio's screams had brought them both running. *If you are so insistent upon it, then I shall tell you the truth.* And somehow he had made that prospect sound so much more like a threat than any genuine simple clearing up of the confusion that still clouded her past.

'Are you cold?'

Rafael's concerned question was unexpected, startling her.

'No, no, I'm fine.'

If he touched her he would know her words for the lie they were. Her skin was alternately burning hot and icy cold, making her feel as if she was in the grip of some unpleasant fever, and she knew that her voice had a quaver that was put there by uneasiness and uncertainty.

'Are you sure?' It was sharper now, demanding an honest answer.

'Perhaps a little tired,' Serena admitted, and heard him curse in soft Spanish.

'*Perdón!* I had completely forgotten you are fresh out of hospital. Let me take Tonio now.'

'It's all right.'

Serena had to struggle to smooth an unexpected sharpness out of her voice. She was strangely reluctant to hand over the little boy to Rafael, unwilling to relinquish the sensation of holding his warm little body snuggled close, to lose the sweet scent of him, the sound of the contented little grunts he made as he sucked at the bottle.

'He's almost finished... There... And what about the wind, young man?' Supporting the baby upright on her knee, she rubbed softly at his back. 'Do you have a—? Oh, yes!'

A bubble of laughter escaped her as Tonio gave a loud burp that shook his small frame, and automatically she looked up into Rafael's face to share the amusement.

But what she saw there had the chuckle dying in her throat, her eyes dropping again swiftly, unable to face the laser-like force of his gaze. He seemed to want to probe right into her mind, into her soul, and read her innermost secrets there.

'Don't!' she whispered, not really knowing what she was asking, what she wanted him not to do.

Beside her she heard Rafael stir slightly, but didn't dare to lift her face to his, and so was startled when she felt a light touch on the hair at the nape of her neck. Gently the strong fingers moved the auburn strands aside, and she sensed rather than saw him bend his head before he kissed her very softly, his lips warm against the delicate skin he had exposed.

Serena froze immediately, her eyes opening wide in shock, her hands stilling on Tonio's back. Rafael's breath whispered entrancing sensations over her sensitised nerves, awakening the need that his lightest touch seemed to spark off, making her pulse start to race as it had done earlier.

But earlier that night everything had seemed so much easier, simpler. Since then she had learned so much that complicated things, changing her perspective.

And so when Rafael lowered his head again she was unable to stop herself from stiffening in rejection.

'Don't!' she gasped again, protestingly.

She was painfully aware of the sudden tautness of the dark figure beside her, the way that one lean, strong hand still lingered on her neck, the bronzed fingers somehow eloquently communicating withdrawal without actually being snatched away.

'*Perdón!*' he said again, but this time with a very different intonation from the one he had used before.

Then he was gone, moving to the opposite side of the room where he propped his long body against the wall and waited in brooding silence as she settled Tonio back in her arms and rocked him gently.

Now at last it seemed the baby was drifting asleep and he stepped forward and spoke again.

'Give him to me now,' he said, and it was an order, not a request, one that Serena did not dare to rebel against.

With a soft sigh she passed the little boy over, lowering him into Rafael's waiting arms, making a small, concerned sound in her throat as Tonio's eyes, heavy with sleep, nevertheless flickered open briefly at the change in his position.

'He's not quite asleep…' she began, but a swift, sidelong glance from those golden eyes silenced her without a word.

'But you have done quite enough.'

He hadn't even raised his voice above conversational level, but he didn't have to. There was enough force behind the comment to tell Serena that any attempt at resistance was useless.

'You should go to bed yourself, you look worn out.'

'I'm okay.'

She hadn't expected it to have any effect on him and it didn't. He simply ignored the protest in her voice, the mutinous set of her jaw.

'You are pale and heavy-eyed, much like Tonio here. Dr Greene would never forgive me if you suffered a relapse on your first day out of her care.'

'But what about Tonio?'

'I will see to him—Serena,' he added, when it seemed she was about to protest further. 'This is not up for debate. You are to go to bed now and get some sleep.'

'You're treating me as if I were just Tonio's age.' Serena's mouth made a small moue of disagreement as she stubbornly remained exactly where she was.

'Right at this moment you are behaving very much as if that were the case,' Rafael retorted sternly. 'But don't think that because I have Tonio to consider I am not likely to enforce my instructions if I have to.'

He meant it too. The light of warning in his eyes left her in no doubt at all about that, and the sudden hiss of his breath inwards on a snatch of impatience made her stomach clench in apprehension at the thought of what she was risking by her rebellion. But still she couldn't make herself move.

She couldn't believe that the night was going to end like this. What had happened to the heady excitement with which it had started out, the conviction that tonight Rafael would become her lover? That, it seemed, had been destroyed by her discovery of Elena's photograph and the ensuing argument. But perhaps even that could have been resolved if Tonio had stayed asleep and they hadn't been interrupted.

She would never know. And now, for tonight at least, it was too late. She didn't know very much about this Rafael Cordoba, this man who had erupted into her life and turned it upside down, but she did know one thing. When his handsome face wore that cold, set, unyielding expression, there was no moving him. She could beg and plead all night, or kick and scream and rail against his decision, but he would never reconsider it.

She might just as well do as he said and accept that tonight was ruined.

'Serena…' Rafael's voice had taken on a distinctly ominous note. '*Bed—now!*'

Rapidly deciding that in this case at least discretion was the better part of valour, Serena got to her feet in a rush, not daring to risk the possible consequences of disobeying.

'Yes, sir!' she exclaimed, snapping her hand up to her face in a mocking salute.

The brief grin that was Rafael's only response flashed on and off like a neon sign, remaining definitely off as he jerked his dark head towards the door in an autocratically silent gesture of command.

'Goodnight,' he said, all too clearly drawing a line under the day and declaring it over.

Just for a moment Serena wondered what would happen if she gave in to the weak, foolish impulse that swept through her, the sudden longing to step forward and press a goodnight kiss on one lean brown cheek. Or perhaps on the sensual softness of that devastating mouth. But she decided she didn't have the nerve to try.

She certainly didn't feel she could face the rejection that she was sure would result from any such action. The mood Rafael was in, all ruthless determination and rigid control, the seductive lover very definitely buried completely out of sight, he was far more likely to repulse her kiss with a violent movement of his head than he was to accept it or respond in any encouraging way.

And besides, she was tired. It had been a long and wearing day, and she had had more than enough of the emotional ups and downs that had drained all her energy from her.

'I'll say goodnight, then,' she said flatly, forcing herself to walk away, heading for her own room.

But she couldn't resist turning back just once, as she reached the doorway. Couldn't make herself actually leave the room without one last look back at this man who had taken such a hold on her heart in such a short space of time.

'Rafae…' she began, but his name died on her lips, shrivelling in a bitter sense of disappointment as she saw that he hadn't even heard her.

His head was turned away, his attention fixed on Tonio, and it was quite obvious that in the space of a couple of moments he had completely and absolutely dismissed her from his mind.

CHAPTER EIGHT

SERENA woke the next morning to a terrible sense of desolation, the reason for which she couldn't immediately place.

Lying back against the soft pillows in the luxurious comfort of the bedroom Rafael had provided for her, she stared up at the ceiling, frowning slightly, trying to understand just why she felt so bad.

As soon as she had stirred, even before she had opened her eyes, the events of the previous night had come rushing back into her thoughts. Living through them once more, she had experienced all over again the buzzing excitement that had filled her at the beginning, the sense of shock at discovering Elena's photograph, and the horror of the other woman's story.

'No,' she sighed aloud, pushing a hand through her burnished hair as she listened to the birdsong starting up outside. 'No, it's not that that's making me feel this way.'

It wasn't even the recollection of the final moments of the night, the obvious and unfeeling dismissal that had had her slinking off to bed like a kicked puppy, the sense of having no place in Rafael's life eating away at her inside like acid. It had been impossible not to contrast the lonely emptiness of her bed with the long, sensual night she had anticipated in Rafael's arms, and she had shed a few silent tears in the darkness.

But this black mood was bleaker, deeper. It came from a deep-rooted sense of loss, a knowledge that something was very, very wrong with her world and she had no idea what. The worst thing about it was the way it brought back to her how she had felt in the week after her mother had died, and that made it doubly distressing.

'You're getting nowhere!' she told herself, speaking the words out loud because they had more emphasis that way. 'Brooding isn't going to help. Get up and get on with something! You're supposed to be looking after Tonio.'

Tonio. The thought of the baby had her flinging back the bedclothes and leaping out of bed. Snatching up the pale green silk robe that matched her nightdress, she pulled it hastily round her, not troubling to fasten the tie belt.

What was happening with Tonio? The house was totally silent, no sound of anyone stirring. Surely the little boy would be awake by now, wanting his first feed of the day. Or had the bottle he had had late in the night meant that he was waking late? Was everything all right?

Nervous and uncertain, her heart lurching into a disturbed beat, she headed out of her room, crossing the corridor swiftly to the baby's room opposite.

In the doorway, she stopped dead in shock. The cot was empty. The brightly coloured quilt had been thrown back, leaving the mattress exposed, and there was no small, sturdy body lying there, gurgling happily or screaming an angry protest as he had been doing last night.

'Tonio?'

A cold hand clutched at her throat. Where was he? What had happened?

But even as panic started to mount she heard a faint sound. A small, snuffling chirrup that she immediately recognised.

Not pausing to consider whether she should or not, she pushed open another door, the one to the room where the sound had come from, and took several hurried steps into the room. Then froze as she realised just what she had done.

This was Rafael's room. Its uncompromisingly masculine navy blue and white decor made that only too plain. And Rafael himself was right there in front of her.

Casually dressed in a black vee neck tee shirt and loose blue trousers, he was sitting cross-legged on the bed. His feet were bare, his hair still slightly ruffled from his night's sleep.

In his arms he held Tonio, the baby's head resting on one bronzed forearm, his dark head bent as he looked down into the baby's face.

The fact that he hadn't heard her come in gave Serena a minute or two to pause and look at the two of them there together.

As always, the contrast between the man's mature, powerful strength and the baby's tiny fragility snatched at her heart, her eyes misting with tears. Right at this moment she couldn't have said which of the two of them had captured her feelings the most. She only knew that in the space of a few short days they had become immeasurably important to her, vital to her life, essential as breathing.

As she watched, Tonio stirred slightly, making a soft, gurgling sound and blowing a small, transparent bubble as he did so. In response, a gentle smile crossed Rafael's face, transforming it completely, and one long finger delicately traced the outline of the baby's face, that smile growing at the little boy's babble of delight.

And it was then that she registered with a shock that was like a blow to her heart the way that the rich black lashes fringing those remarkable eyes looked so very different. No longer soft and separate, they were clumped into spikes, clinging together damply.

Serena recognised that look. It was the way her own eyes seemed after a bout of weeping, and her heart clenched in distress as she saw the telltale shadows under Rafael's eyes, the faint revealing marks on his skin. Recalling her own angry words of the previous night, the accusations she had flung at him, the way she had been convinced he wasn't even capable of mourning his dead love, Serena felt guilt twist painfully in her stomach.

She should go, she told herself silently. She should leave the pair of them together and not intrude on this very private, very personal moment. But as she was turning away she didn't notice that the tie belt belonging to her robe was trailing on the floor, snaking under her feet. Her toes tangled up in it and she stumbled awkwardly, her hand going out to the door for support.

Immediately Rafael's dark head came up, golden eyes flashing towards her, black brows drawing together in a swift frown. A frown that, disconcertingly, didn't lighten when he saw Serena standing in the doorway.

'B-Buenos días,' she stammered awkwardly, switching on a smile to try and lighten the atmosphere.

There was no returning smile in response, only a cold, unblinking stare that made her stomach twist into knots of apprehension and uncertainty

'That's right, isn't it?' she tried again. 'Buenos días does mean good morning?'

'Yes, it does.' Rafael's voice seemed to come from a long, long way away. 'Buenos días, querida.'

The last word, with its implication of affection, was said on such a note of irony that it stripped away any warmth from the term, leaving it instead as something close to an insult. But it wasn't that that brought Serena's hand up to her face, covering her mouth to conceal the gasp of shock that escaped her.

In the moment that Rafael had spoken something had clicked in her mind. It had been like a light switch going on, illuminating some previously hidden and shadowy corner of her thoughts, revealing them with an almost shocking clarity.

'A dream!' she whispered, her voice shaking and disturbed. 'It was a dream.'

'¿Cómo?' Rafael questioned, frowning, but Serena could only shake her head in distress, unable to answer him.

Like brief, disjointed scenes from a film, images were playing over in her mind, flashing into focus briefly, then blurring into confusion once again.

'I had a dream last night.'

She shook her head again, her eyes dark with confusion as she struggled to make sense of things.

'It was dark—night time—I—I was in a car...'

'*Dios!*'

She had his full attention now. Carefully depositing Tonio on the bed, a cushion at either side of the small body to make sure he didn't roll off, Rafael came to her side. With a small, fluttering, imploring movement of her hands, she turned to him, wanting to touch him, to be held. But he held his lean body tautly away from her, his face set sternly, his eyes distant.

'A car,' he repeated, his voice sounding like the bite of a cruel trap. 'What car?'

'I—I don't know. A black car. Long, low—the seats were cream leather...'

Rafael swore violently. '*El mio coche,*' he muttered, bringing her shocked eyes to his face in a rush.

'*Mio*—you mean it was *your* car. The car I had the accident in?'

'The same. What else did you dream?'

'I...'

'Serena!' The Spanish Inquisitor was back, with a vengeance. 'What else did you dream?'

'It's all so muddled—so confused.'

Serena pressed her hands to her head, covering her eyes as she struggled to concentrate.

She could picture the darkness of the night, the glare of powerful headlights on the road in front of them. The movement of the car was sickening, the speed terrifying, the reckless way it swung round corners, negotiated obstacles frankly insane. Obscured by the roar of the engine, someone was begging, pleading, and another voice, a cold, angry voice...

'*You!*'

Serena's thoughts reeled and she rounded on Rafael, her eyes just deep brown pools of shock in her ashen, pallid face.

'It was you! You were the driver.'

'*Madre de Dios!*' Rafael threw up his hands in a gesture

of furious exasperation. 'I thought that you were beginning
to remember.'

'I was! I was…'

Her protest shrivelled in the force of the violently scathing
look he flung at her, the brief moment of hope, the sensation
of finally getting somewhere deflating rapidly like a pricked
balloon.

'I thought I was,' she amended miserably. 'You said the
car was right.'

'You described my car correctly,' Rafael agreed. 'But if
you saw me in the driving seat, then I can assure you that
you are not remembering but fantasising.'

Serena's head drooped despondently, her eyes clouding.
She was reluctant to let the images go. Taking them together
with the terrible sense of desolation that had tormented her
from the moment that she had woken, they had seemed to
be her best chance of remembering the lost year of her life.
But if Rafael said…

Suddenly her head came up again sharply, sending the
silky coppery hair swinging around a face that had regained
some faint degree of colour.

'Do you *want* me to remember?' she challenged.

'Of course.'

His response came swiftly, almost instantly, and to all but
the closest of observers his assertion had all the confidence
of absolute truth. But, abnormally sensitive to everything
about him, every tiny flicker of emotion across his handsome
face, every nuance and tone in the softly accented voice,
Serena was suddenly not totally convinced.

She was sure that she had caught a momentary hesitation,
a fractional change in his manner, and those heavy lids had
dropped for the briefest of pauses, hiding the expression in
the bright eyes behind the luxuriant curtain of long black
lashes.

'That's what you say! But how can I trust you? You told
me you weren't even in England at the time, but I have only

your word for that. I don't *know* that it's true! You claimed that the man driving the car was—'

'I did not *claim*,' Rafael inserted dangerously, eyes black with cold rage. 'I told you...'

'Oh, I know what you told me, but quite frankly you could have told me anything you liked! You could have claimed that I was your wife and Tonio my child if you'd wanted! If you'd told me I was driving that car I would have to believe you because I have nothing else to put in its place.'

Her violent outburst had driven Rafael to curl his hands into tightly clenched fists at his side, evidence of the struggle he was having to keep a grip on a temper that was definitely beginning to fray at the edges. But Serena was beyond heeding the warning implicit in his reaction, too wound up to care what he thought of her.

'How do I know that you're not lying to cover things up?'

'What sort of things?' Rafael rapped out, golden eyes narrowing sharply until they were just slits in his tanned face.

Trying desperately to think of something, Serena snatched at the first idea that came to her.

'Well, it could have been you that was driving the car, you that caused the...'

His genuine amusement was the last thing she had expected. Stunned into silence, she could only stand and watch him throw back his dark head and laugh out loud, his teeth very white against the bronze tan of his skin.

'What?' she demanded indignantly when at last she had recovered the nerve to speak.

'Oh, Serena, *querida*...' Rafael drawled lazily, laughter still warming his voice.

But this time it was not the good-humoured amusement of a moment before. Instead, it had a sardonic, mocking quality to it that scraped nastily over Serena's already sensitised nerves.

'Now I know that you are not thinking straight, *belleza*. If I truly had been driving the car, as it seems I was in your wild, irrational fantasy, do you really believe that your wonderful police force—the so efficient British bobby—would not have worked that out by now? Do you not think that they might have—?'

'Okay, okay, I get the picture!' Serena snapped. 'So you weren't driving the car! I concede that. And—and the driver—the real driver—he truly is dead?'

Abruptly Rafael's mood sobered completely, every trace of laughter draining from his face, leaving it pale and shadowed.

'Sí,' he confirmed with sombre reluctance. 'He was killed outright.'

Serena's hands fretted at the belt of her robe, twisting the green silk round and round in her hands, tangling it around her fingers.

'I still think I should have done something...'

'No!' It was hard, inflexible, absolute, leaving no room for argument. 'I told you there was nothing you could do. Nothing that would have been in the slightest bit welcome.'

'But just the same—'

She was interrupted by a cry from the bed. Bored with staring at the ceiling and watching his own small hands waving in the air, Tonio was intent on reminding them of his presence. Immediately both Serena and Rafael were all attention.

'What is it, poppet?' Serena crooned, bending over him in concern, much to the baby's delight, as he found a new and fascinating diversion in the silken strands of her coppery hair. 'Are you hungry?'

'Not at all,' Rafael declared. 'I'd only just given him his bottle when you came in.'

With a wave of his hand he indicated the empty container, unnoticed until now on the bedside table.

'But if things follow their usual pattern, then I strongly suspect that, having filled up at one end, he has made a space at the other. He probably needs changing—I'll leave that pleasure to you.'

'Thanks!' Serena returned dryly, glad to be distracted from the uncomfortable topic of their earlier conversation. Reaching for the little boy, she lifted him from his nest on the bed. 'I'll see to him straight away.'

'You might want to fasten yourself up first,' Rafael surprised her by saying. 'You wouldn't want to fall while you were carrying him.'

Following the direction of his eyes, she looked down at herself. A small cry of shock escaped her, hot colour rushing up into her cheeks as she realised how the mint-green robe hung loosely open, revealing the low-cut vee neck and ribbon straps of the matching nightdress. Far too much creamy skin was exposed to view, the rich curves of her breasts pushing against the delicate silk in a way that was more provocatively sensual than she had ever realised.

The thought that this was how Rafael had seen her from the first moment that he had looked up to find her in the doorway, that this was how she had looked all through the argument about her dream, made her pulse leap in embarrassed consternation.

'You might have told me!' she accused, struggling to pull the sides of her robe together while still holding tight to Tonio's small, warm body.

'I was enjoying the view,' Rafael drawled smoothly, darkened eyes flirting with her outrageously as he watched her efforts, his sensual mouth quirking up at the corners in obvious appreciation of the way that exertion brought a wash of colour to the pallor of her exposed skin. 'And really you have no need to panic. You are revealing nothing more than you would if you were on a beach or—'

'This is not a beach!' Serena snapped, furiously aware of the way that her movements were achieving nothing productive. Instead they were offering him an even better view of the soft sway of her breasts, the writhe of her hips as she squirmed and wriggled in an attempt to restore her appearance to some degree of modesty.

She doubted if she would feel any better if they were actually on a beach or if the flimsy nightdress was a more substantial cotton sundress. The cause of her embarrassment wasn't in what she was wearing or how much of her body was exposed, but in Rafael's reaction. It was there in the unconcealed gleam in his eyes, the frank appreciation of his smile, the all too knowing look he directed at her face. She was well aware of just what thoughts were running through his mind, because they were the same ones as were uppermost in hers.

It seemed somehow close to indecent to have a mind filled with erotic images of Rafael's hands on her skin, of that beautifully soft mouth pressing heated kisses onto even more heated flesh and being held so very, very close to the hard strength of that glorious body, when all the time she held his three-month-old son in her arms.

'Here...' Rafael moved forward suddenly. 'Let me help.'

'Thanks!' Serena acknowledged his belated gesture, only to swallow her appreciation back down again quickly when she realised exactly what he had in mind.

She had thought that he was planning on taking Tonio from her so that she could have both hands free to adjust her clothing and cover herself up. Instead, she found that *he* was intent on being the one doing the adjusting, taking full advantage of the fact that, with Tonio in her arms, she could do nothing to stop him from letting his hands wander at will.

She had no option but to stand, impotently fuming, as he pulled the front of the robe across her breasts, his fingertips carefully and, she was sure, deliberately positioned so that they brushed softly over the swell of her breasts, making the delicate flesh tighten in response. As she swallowed hard, fighting for control, beneath the silk her sensitive nipples peaked, pushing against the material in provocative response. She was perfectly certain that Rafael could not be unaware of her reaction, but he made no comment, seemingly intent on arranging the sit of the robe to his absolute satisfaction. This, of course, involved him in much smoothing and stroking, the warmth of his palms burning an erotic trail everywhere they touched, making her clench her teeth hard against the shuddering response that seemed to come from way down in her soul.

When the top was adjusted to his satisfaction, those tormenting hands moved lower, and a new wave of torment began. A pretence of adjusting the back too meant a similar procedure, a similar sensuously tormenting caress of her buttocks that reduced her insides to a molten mass of nerves, her legs to a quivering jelly. She didn't know how she felt the control not to sway her hips, press her bottom against the cup of his hands, increasing the delicious agony he was already subjecting to.

If her arms had been free and she hadn't had the safety of the baby to consider, she told herself she would have lashed out with an angry hand, wiping that half-absorbed, half-provocative look from his face, the challenging tilt from his mouth once and for all. But even as she let the thought into her mind stern realism pushed it out again.

Who was she trying to kid? She wouldn't have stopped him if she could. Because she could have done it just as efficiently with a few well-chosen words, and she hadn't even managed to open her mouth, except to let that involuntary, shocked gasp of reaction escape at first.

Her heart was beating double-quick time, her breathing matching its uneven patter. Her skin was on fire and the golden haze that blurred her vision would not clear, no matter how many times or how hard she blinked. And just when she thought the erotic ordeal was over, Rafael took hold of both ends of the tie belt, knotting them firmly around her waist with a movement that once again tantalised the still-tingling under-slopes of her breasts.

At long last, after what had seemed like a sensuous lifetime, Rafael released her and stepped backwards. Immediately the fire of need was transformed into a fury of frustration, one that pushed her into hurried speech without pausing to think.

'Satisfied?' she demanded tartly, realising her mistake, the pit she had dug for herself a second too late, so that it was impossible to step backwards from it.

Rafael's slow, wicked grin made it clear that he was well aware of the unfortunate choice of words, and had no intention at all of letting her off the hook.

'Satisfied?' he drawled sardonically, and the light of demonic amusement made his eyes glow. 'Far from it, *querida*. I would much rather be taking this seductive sliver of material *off* your delectable body, sliding it from you as I would peel the soft skin from a sun-ripened peach, revealing—'

'I'm afraid all you're revealing are your own overblown, very macho fantasies,' Serena inserted tartly, unable to take any more of this deliberately sexual provocation. 'And if you don't stop drooling and let me get on with other, far more practical matters then I'm afraid that the other man in my life is going to make his uncomfortable feelings only too vociferously plain.'

'The other...?' For a moment Rafael looked confused.

'I'm talking about Tonio,' Serena elucidated firmly. 'If he didn't need changing when you started on all this nonsense then he does now—and if my sense of smell is anything to go by, then the matter is very definitely verging on urgent.'

'In that case...' Rafael stepped back hastily. 'You'd better get on with it.'

'See, poppet.' Serena addressed the baby in her arms in an audible stage whisper as she flounced past Rafael on her way to the nursery. 'Daddy does have a brain cell in his head sometimes. One that isn't totally obsessed with the region below his belt. I'm sure when you grow up—'

'When he grows up...' Rafael's voice came down the corridor after her '...I'm sure he'll find the female form every bit as enchanting and delightful as I do.'

'Of course he will!' Serena tossed over her shoulder with a swift glance back at his tall, dark form as it lounged in the doorway of his bedroom. 'After all he is your son and heir. And like father, like son.'

But she'd overstepped the mark somewhere there, she realised as the smile that had curved that sensual mouth vanished rapidly, stormclouds gathering on Rafael's stunning features.

'You were employed to take care of Tonio,' he snapped with an abrupt change of mood. 'Not to pass comment on my character and the way I live my life. I'd appreciate it if you'd remember that. When you've changed him and cleaned him up, put him down in his cot. It's time for his nap.'

'Yes, sir!' Serena saluted smartly before disappearing into the baby's room where she laid him down on the padded changing mat, smiling down into his upturned face.

'Well, I wonder what rattled Daddy's cage,' she said, half-laughing, half-disturbed by Rafael's sudden change of mood. 'Any ideas?'

But Tonio simply regarded her with wide, unblinking golden eyes and blew a happy bubble, waving his arms and legs wildly in the air as she began to unfasten his sleepsuit.

Some fifteen minutes later, with Tonio cleaned, changed and lying happily in his cot, already halfway towards being asleep, Serena made her way back to her room, thinking longingly of a long hot shower, a chance to wash her hair, and finally to get dressed to face the day.

Was it really not even two hours since she had woken that morning? It seemed more than twice as long as that since she had first opened her eyes to that dreadfully oppressive sense of apprehension.

Recalling that moment, she frowned, slumping down in front of the dressing table and surveying her reflection in the mirror ruefully, noting the still shadowed eyes, the marks of the restless night that showed on her skin. In the back of her mind the images of her dream still lingered, like sticky, dirty cobwebs, clinging to her thoughts and tainting her pleasure in the day.

'I was so sure!' she muttered out loud. 'So sure it was a memory and not just a dream.'

But any suspicion she had had that Rafael had indeed been the driver of the car had vanished in the face of his laughter. His amusement had been genuine, his scorn obvious. In that at least her dream had totally misled her. So what had led her to even think that Rafael might have been the man at the wheel, the man who had crashed the car?

The truth was that the dream had been unclear from start to finish. The car had been in almost total darkness, her eyes blinded by the blaze of the headlights.

Sighing, Serena rested her chin on her elbows and stared into the darkened eyes of her own face in the mirror.

'So why, why did it happen?' she asked herself. 'Why on earth should I dream about Rafael of all people?'

'That's easy to answer.'

The low, huskily accented voice came from behind her, bringing her eyes up in a rush to see reflected in the mirror Rafael's tall, powerful form as he lounged in the open doorway, one long-fingered hand resting negligently against its wooden frame.

'You see, *querida*,' he went on, when she could find no response but could only remain frozen, staring into the mirror, watching him silently through the glass. 'It comes as no surprise to find that you have been dreaming about me. After all, I have spent so much time lying awake at nights just thinking of you. And we both know why that is.'

'Oh, do we?' Serena's tongue felt thick and clumsy and she had to force herself into speech.

He didn't condescend to answer, obviously not thinking the question worth the effort of a response as he straightened up, flexing his broad shoulders with the slow, indolent grace of a hunting tiger. The single silent step he took into the room was enough to startle her into action, leaping to her feet and whirling round to face him, bright hair flying round her face, her eyes wide and startled, like those of a wary deer facing the predator that had it cornered.

'Exactly what do you mean?'

'Oh, come now, *mi belleza*.'

Rafael's shake of his dark head was slow, frankly sceptical, expressing total disbelief in her claim not to understand.

'You know just what I mean. I have been dreaming of you because, from the moment I first set eyes on you, you have stirred my senses like no other woman I have ever encountered. I want you so much it's like an ache in my guts, an ache that's always there, day or night, sleeping or waking. That's why I dream of you—hot, hungry dreams that promise so much and yet deliver nothing. When I wake up, the ache— the hunger—is still there, worse than ever because I came so close...'

His eyes locked with hers, the golden brilliance almost totally obscured by the inky black of his enlarged pupils, so that they had taken on the appearance of an eclipsed sun, with only the finest corona of colour showing in their darkness.

'And you understand this because it is exactly the same for you.'

'N...'

Fearfully Serena opened her mouth to answer him, to refute the accusation, only to find that her voice failed her completely, managing only a faint, incomprehensible murmur. Swallowing desperately, she ran a nervous tongue along her painfully dry lips and tried again, with exactly the same unproductive result. No matter how much her mind screamed a command to deny him, loud and clear, it seemed that her mouth was absolutely incapable of speaking what she knew only too well was a total lie.

'Yes,' Rafael declared thickly, the powerful emphasis on the word sounding the death knell for any hope she might have had of convincing him he was mistaken. 'You know what I've been going through because you've dreamed of me, wanted me, *ached* for me just as I have ached for you. Shall I tell you about my dreams, Serena?'

'No-o-o.'

This time she actually managed to get the denial out, a sense of near panic turning it into a long drawn-out moan of something close to despair.

The night before she had dreamed of just such a moment as this; dreamed of Rafael coming to her, a passionate, ardent lover, with words of fire on his tongue to match the desire in his heart. But now that her dream had become reality she was forced to face the fact that it came trailing very bitter strings indeed.

Because Rafael wasn't offering her his *heart*. There was nothing of emotion, no feeling in what he wanted from her, and in return he was prepared to give nothing beyond the purely physical. In the short space of time that she had known him, he and little Tonio had burrowed so deeply into her own heart that she knew she would never be able to break free from them again. But for Rafael the sexual desire he felt for her had always been the beginning and the end of it.

'No, Rafael,' she tried again, her voice rough and uneven. But he wasn't listening to her.

'Shall I tell you how you come to me—naked and warm— so warm that it's like a fire licking along my skin? How you twine your arms around me, tangle your fingers in my hair, kiss me and kiss me until my head is spinning and the only thing I can think of is you?'

'Rafael, please...' Serena whispered, and saw his quick, dangerously enticing smile.

'Do you know how many times I've heard you say that in my dreams? How I've heard you murmur it in my ear, heard you beg me to take you, to make love to you until we're both so drained that even to breathe is an effort. And do you know what it does to me to wake and find that none of it was true? That it was a fantasy, a hallucination created by my own imagination? Can you imagine what that is like?'

'Oh, yes!'

The confession was dragged out of her, forced from her lips by the memory of the dream she had had in the hospital, and again, here in this room, last night. The memory of the dream and the way it had felt to wake and find that it was unreal, the dreadful dragging emptiness it had left behind.

'I knew it.'

Rafael's voice was like a tiger's purr, rich with a dark, savage triumph.

'I knew that was how it would be for you too. But not any more. Today is the day we put an end to dreaming. Today, Serena, *mi corazón*, we find out if reality can match up to the fantasy.'

And, moving fully into the room at last, he kicked the door shut behind him.

CHAPTER NINE

'RAFAEL…'

It was a protest, an entreaty and an enticement all rolled into one.

'Rafael, I don't think I can do this.'

His smile was a swift upward quirk of his lips, there and gone in the space of a heartbeat. It was coldly amused, faintly cruel, no trace of genuine warmth in the golden shards of ice that were his eyes.

'Oh, Serena…'

The intensity of his mood had also heightened his accent so that her name came out as *Serrreynya*, the strangely exotic sound of it making her bare toes curl convulsively on the rich, soft carpet.

'Serena, *mi amor*, thinking is precisely what you must not do. The time for thought is past. Now we put what we have both been thinking into action. And besides, I want my revenge.'

Serena's head came up sharply, deep brown eyes opening wide in shock.

'R-revenge?' She hadn't expected this and the thought was frankly terrifying.

This time his smile was wide and slow and sexy, pure, arrogant cat who had the cream in his sights and fully intended to enjoy every last drop of it.

'You accused me of some unspeakable things. Of having only one brain cell, one that concentrated on my own pleasure. Of drooling… *Madre de Dios!*'

His eyes flashed, aristocratic nostrils flaring in haughty disgust at the idea.

'I have never *drooled* over anyone in my life! And I do

114

not intend to start now. And as to thinking only of my-self…you owe me the chance to prove you wrong. Come to me, *mi corazón*…'

One lean brown hand was held out, inviting her to put hers into it, and Serena's throat dried painfully at just the thought of the warmth and strength of those long, hard fingers closing firmly about her own.

'Come to me and let me prove to you how, when I am with you, I can think of nothing *but* you. How I can kiss you in so many different ways that you will never, ever tire of it. How I can touch you, caress you, until your body burns up in my arms and your mind melts in the heat of it. I will teach you things you never knew about yourself, find pleasure spots you had no idea even existed…'

Her body was burning up already, and he was only *talking* to her! Serena admitted dazedly. She didn't dare to try to imagine what the reality would be like when he actually ful-filled his promise.

And her mind must be melting too, because she didn't recall having taken a single step forward, and yet somehow the gap between them had closed and she was only just a few short inches away from him, that arrogantly summoning hand now almost touching her face.

'Come to me…' His voice had dropped a husky octave so that it coiled around her heightened senses like warm, intox-icating smoke. 'Come to me and let me show you what mak-ing love is really like.'

'Rafael…'

It was a sigh of surrender, of longing. Unable to deny her own feelings any longer, she moved swiftly, but not to take the hand he held out. Instead, she flung herself across the small expanse of carpet that still separated them, her arms coming up and encircling his neck, linking at the base of his skull to draw his proud, dark head down to hers. Then, with the soft sensuality of his mouth only agonising inches away from her own, she paused to look up into his face, deep brown eyes clashing with molten amber ones.

'You'd better be able to deliver what you promise!' she told him, her voice rasping in the urgency of her need.

With her gaze so firmly locked onto the golden blaze of his, she couldn't see his smile, but she watched its reflection warm and colour his eyes, like the sun rising over the horizon at the start of a sultry summer day.

'You have my word on that,' he promised deeply, his words as husky as hers had been. 'Everything I promised, you shall have. Everything—and more.'

And then his dark head came down, his mouth plundering hers, and immediately the first of his promises was fulfilled. One kiss, and she was incapable of thought, her rational capabilities destroyed as easily and surely as a bolt of lightning landing a direct hit could burn up the most complicated electrical system, fusing all the delicate and complicated wiring into one unusable, liquefied pool of heat.

Yesterday she had had such doubts; even just such a short time before the conviction that this was wrong, that it was not for her, had overwhelmed her. But she had no time for any such feelings now. Now she was starving, faint with hunger, and Rafael was offering her the sort of banquet that she no longer had the strength to resist.

His mouth on hers was pure seduction. One moment it was all heat and fire, demanding and plundering, until her head swam and her fingers clenched over the tight, hard muscles in his powerful shoulders. But somehow he had an intuitive sense of the split second before such forcefulness became intolerable, never letting her reach it. Instead he gentled his caress, turning it into a kiss of such sweetness, such delicacy that it twisted something sharply deep at her most feminine inner core.

Hot tears burned in her eyes, slid out from under her closed lids as she surrendered to a sensation that seemed capable of drawing her soul out of her body. Her heart seemed to have stopped beating altogether as he moved fluidly against her, drawing her into intimate contact with the heated thrust of his arousal.

'You see what you do to me?' he muttered roughly against her tingling mouth. 'See the power you have over me?'

'Power?' Serena choked, unable to believe his choice of words. It seemed to her that he was the one with all the power, the one in control, his innate physical strength combining with her own yearning need to create a potent, voluptuous force that was impossible to resist. 'I don't...'

'But you do,' he assured her huskily. 'You have the power to take me to heaven or consign me to hell. To drive me mad with hunger or to fulfil my wildest fantasies...the first one of which is this...'

Impatient hands tugged at the tie belt on her robe, letting it fall softly open, the heat of his touch trailing paths of fire as he smoothed it from her body to fall in a soft green pool at her feet. Serena shivered as the fine material slid over her skin, but it was anticipation and not fear that made her body tremble. She had never felt so vibrantly, powerfully alive, the exciting sensations his touch sparked off in her racing through every cell in her body like some crackling electrical current, tantalising every inch of her skin.

'Rafael...'

She wanted to tell him. Wanted him to know how she felt, the effect he was having on her. But her tongue seemed to have seized up and there was no way she could put into words the sweetly savage hunger that was spiralling deep inside, uncoiling swiftly and gloriously like some brilliant, golden Catherine wheel, sending flares of heat licking along every vein, melting her blood.

'Rafael...' she tried again.

'What is it?'

The warmth of his whisper against the sensitivity of her skin was another delightful torment, a further intensification of the fizzing excitement that was reducing her body to a state of mindless, yearning need.

'Kiss...' She couldn't voice the longing coherently.

But he had no need of any instructions. Interpreting her stumbling cries with an intuitive accuracy that was almost telepathic, he slid the heat of his mouth away from her lips and down the long slender line of her throat. Pausing to press a burning kiss over the frantic pulse that beat in the hollow at the base of her neck, he used his lips and tongue, even his teeth, nibbling delicately at the soft skin of her shoulders and the tops of her arms.

'This is what you want,' he asserted thickly, his voice rich with the certainty of his understanding. 'This...'

His tongue lapped at the exposed upper slopes of her breasts.

'And this...'

That tormenting mouth slid lower, its heated caress combining with the gentle slide of silk over the sensitive curves to create an erotic friction that made her senses swim in ecstasy.

'Yes...' Serena sighed. 'Oh, yes.'

From uncertainty and apprehension she had now moved into a mood of abandonment, of total submission to his lovemaking.

She could trust him completely with her body, she knew. Trust him to make love to her with all the ardour and desire of which his passionate nature was capable. Trust him to teach her the sensual magic that the two of them could create between them, a magic that she could find nowhere else but with him.

But, most of all, she knew she could put herself entirely in his hands, into his control, and know that he would take her to the greatest heights of pleasure. That he would give her the gratification she yearned for, the glowing fulfilment he had promised her.

But still she couldn't hold back, couldn't stop herself from urging him on.

'More...' she muttered, her own voice thickening with hunger as his already had. 'More...' And felt the warm breath of his laughter like an additional caress.

'Oh, you shall have more, *querida*,' he promised huskily. 'You shall have more and more and more, until you think you'll die from the glory of it. What would you like me to do? Kiss you here?'

Warm, strong hands cupped her breasts through the fine green silk, lifting them to the heat of his mouth. Serena flung her burnished head back in involuntary response, a wild, uncontrollable cry escaping her as he circled one peaking nipple with his tongue, moistening the delicate material until it clung to her responsive flesh, revealing the tightness, the subtle hardening that was her body's urgent response to him.

Taking the swollen peak into his mouth through the tautness of the fabric, he sucked on it strongly, bringing a sharp, stinging pleasure that had her writhing in agonised delight against the virile strength of his body. Her hands clutched at the dark silk of his hair, she crushed her hips against his pelvis, drawing a raw, primitive groan from deep in his throat as she moved sinuously over the heated evidence of his sexual hunger.

'*Dios!*' Rafael muttered roughly, the hoarseness of the word evidence of how close he was to losing what little control was left to him. 'This has to go—I want you naked...'

The green nightdress was wrenched from her body and tossed carelessly into some other part of the room where it fell unheeded onto the floor. Rafael's hands became her only covering, touching, stroking, teasing, drawing wildly erotic patterns on her skin before finally sliding even lower to dance tormentingly close to the burning centre of her desire but never quite touching until she was gritting her teeth against screaming in frustration.

'*Rafael!*'

This time it was an angry protest as, lacing her fingers in his hair to hold him captive, she crushed her mouth to his in a hungry demonstration of just what he was doing to her. The aching tips of her breasts were pressed against the black cotton of his tee shirt, making her yearn for the heated caress of flesh against flesh.

'You are wearing too many clothes!' she muttered complainingly.

'Am I indeed?'

Wickedly golden eyes gleamed into hers, recognising how close she was to breaking, acknowledging the hunger that matched his own.

'That is easily remedied.'

His hands went to the hem of the tee shirt, pulling it loose from the leather belt at his narrow waist.

'No... Let me.'

This way she could have her revenge for the way that he had tortured her, Serena resolved, deliberately taking her time about sliding the black tee shirt from his powerful body. She let her fingertips trail over the heated silk of his torso, smiling in pure feminine mastery as she watched the powerful muscles bunch and clench under the bronze skin, heard his rawly indrawn gasps of pleasure.

But when her hands dropped to the buckle of his belt he stilled completely. Taut with expectation, he waited silently as she eased it open, teasingly matching his own movements earlier when he had smoothed the green silk robe over her hips. Her fingers shook slightly as she found the zip on his trousers, slid it downwards, then moved inwards, smoothing aside the silk shorts he wore, releasing the heated power of his manhood into her waiting grasp.

'*Maldito sea!*'

His command of the English language deserting him in the same moment that his control snapped completely, Rafael kicked himself free of the last restraints of his clothing and reached for her urgently.

Sweeping her up off her feet and into his arms, he carried her the few feet across the room to the bed, tumbling her onto it with a lack of care that demonstrated only too clearly how close he was to letting go completely. Coming swiftly down beside her, he inserted one muscular brown leg between her slender white thighs, pushing them apart and opening her up to him.

And then she did feel his touch where she most ached for it. Felt hard, knowing fingers move purposefully to tease, to caress, to awaken the deepest yearning she had ever known, to drive her almost to the edge but not quite over it.

Her mind adrift on a sea of sensation, her whole body an agony of hunger, Serena reached for him desperately, wanting him, needing the force of his possession so violently that she thought she would break apart if he didn't take her now.

'Yes,' she muttered feverishly. 'Rafael, yes…yes…'

But unbelievably, shockingly, Rafael had stilled, the unexpectedness of his change of mood like a cruel blow to her heart.

'Rafael…?'

Suddenly fearful, she opened passion-blurred eyes and tried to focus on his dark, set face just above her.

'Rafael, what is it?'

'Serena, *mi corazón*,' he muttered, his voice shaking as much as the hands that cupped her face. 'Be sure—be very sure that this is what you want. If you think for one moment that you will regret his—that you will wish it had never happened—then stop me now. Stop it while I can still think, still—'

'No!'

Breaking free of his hold, she reared up slightly to crush her mouth to his, stopping the flow of muttered words.

'No!' she repeated, more insistently this time. 'No, I won't regret this. No, I could never wish it hadn't happened. And most of all no, no, *no*, I do not want you to stop.'

'Dios gracias!' The exclamation had all the fervency of a heartfelt prayer. *'Dios gracias,* because neither do I.'

And, capturing her mouth with his once again, he slid his hands underneath her, cupping her buttocks and tilting her up towards him. He entered her swiftly in one wild, fierce thrust that drew a cry of shocked delight from both of them in stunned communion, their eyes wide open, staring deep into each other's faces as he began to move.

The flare of response deep inside her was instantaneous, blazing through her until she felt she could take no more. But there was more to come, and Rafael controlled it every inch of the way. Each hard, hot thrust of his powerful body was designed to take her higher, higher, higher, until at last she reached the point where her control shattered and she arced convulsively against him, his name a wild moan of rapture on her lips as she surrendered totally to blazing, incandescent pleasure.

She didn't know how long it was before the last of the shuddering, convulsive aftershocks eased from her body and her mind began to function again. She only knew that the reality she returned to was not the same as the one she had left behind, and never would be again.

Reality now was the fact that Rafael was her lover, and that was the path she must follow, no matter what it brought to her. And, as he had declared to her earlier, he now had the power to take her to heaven or consign her to the depths of hell. Because this man who had taken her body to such heights of passion, who had shown her the true meaning of pleasure, had also taken her heart. She had fallen totally, irredeemably and hopelessly in love with Rafael Cordoba, and because of that her life would never, ever be truly hers again.

Beside her she felt Rafael stir lazily, his sigh an expression of deep contentment. Too aware of her own new feelings, and so too vulnerable to open her eyes and meet that searching, brilliant gaze, she reached out a hand and touched him lightly on the arm.

'I'll say one thing for you,' she murmured, managing what she hoped was a careless smile. 'When you make a promise, you certainly deliver.'

She couldn't see his answering smile but she heard it in his voice when he murmured, his tone low and huskily sensual, 'I pride myself on the fact that when I give my word I always keep it. And here's another promise for you. Whatever you felt this time, believe me, it was only the beginning. We have some long, long nights ahead of us, *querida*. Nights in which I aim to show you what passion really means.'

That promise was to linger in Serena's mind throughout the following week, often making her lips curve into a warmly sensual smile when she thought of it. By the end of that time she could be in no doubt at all that Rafael had meant exactly what he had said.

Every night brought a new delight, a new variation on sensuality, an added refinement that heightened pleasure to peaks she had never known it could reach, taught her things she had never known about her own sexuality, revealed a power of passion she had never dreamed existed. And every day her love for Rafael grew to match her desire for him until, by the end of seven short days and seven very long nights, she knew he was as essential to her as the beat of her heart, the air she breathed.

But sometimes when she acknowledged this truth to herself her smile would slip and dark shadows would cloud her eyes. Because although Rafael made it plain that, right now, she was a vital, central part of his life, the ardent physical passion he showed her was as far as it went. He made no avowals of feeling, promised nothing, never even seemed to consider that she might dream of more. What he had was enough for him, and he seemed to believe it should be enough for her too.

And there was still the problem of her memory. The missing twelve months that were locked away in her mind stayed firmly hidden, impossible to access. She was no nearer to discovering what had happened to her in that time than in the first moments when she had woken in the hospital after her accident.

So she felt a thrill of anticipation, a sudden renewal of hope, when Rafael came home one afternoon with some unexpected and exciting news.

'Does this mean anything to you?' he asked, holding out a piece of paper with a couple of lines of writing on it.

The supremely casual, almost throwaway tone of voice didn't deceive Serena, and she almost snatched the note out of his grip. But, after scanning the address it contained, she felt the all too familiar kickback of disappointment at the realisation that it was totally unknown to her.

Despondently she shook her head.

'I don't recognise it at all. Why? Should it mean something to me?'

His golden eyes were coolly assessing, narrowed thoughtfully as he watched her, obviously noting every last detail of her reaction and storing it away for future reference.

'I'm told that it's the address you lived at in London. The place you were staying before the accident.'

'It is?'

Grabbing the note back again, she read it over and over, dwelling on each component of it, trying desperately to drag some knowledge, some memory out of the neat black letters. But nothing happened. The address remained no more than a string of words written on a page. She couldn't visualise a house to go with the details, didn't even recognise the district of London.

'I know nothing about this Norway Street,' she sighed. 'It doesn't mean a thing. How did you find out about it?'

'From a detective I hired.'

Rafael's face was expressionless. If he had shared her excitement or her disappointment it didn't show in the cool, slightly distant eyes, the carefully schooled features.

'I've had him working on the case for a while now.'

'You never told me!'

'There was nothing to tell. And there was no point in you getting excited or tense until there was something to show for his work.'

'This address is the first thing he's discovered?'

'The first thing of any importance to you. But perhaps it's something of a dead end.'

'It can't be!'

Serena's fingers clenched tightly over the small piece of paper as if it was a lifeline, which right now it seemed to her that it was. It was her only link with an existence she couldn't remember.

'Surely we can do something with this. We can go there—investigate this address, see what we can find.'

Rafael clearly didn't share her enthusiasm, his beautiful mouth twisting in obvious distaste.

'This is not one of the smartest districts in London,' he said with obvious understatement. 'I understand that Norway Street is *un barrio bajo*—a slum.'

'I don't care if it's the end of the world!' Serena asserted, refusing to be put off. 'It has some connection with my past and I want to see it.'

CHAPTER TEN

'WELL, I warned you.'

Rafael switched off the car's engine and turned in his seat, sharp tawny eyes taking in the shocked expression on Serena's face.

'I did tell you...'

'I know what you told me, but I hadn't expected this...' The hand that she waved towards the dilapidated house was distinctly unsteady. 'This *dump*! Are you sure we've got the right address?'

'Perfectly sure.'

Rafael's tone was crisp and cool. Ever since she had declared her intention of seeing Norway Street for herself he had seemed to step back from her, mentally at least, maintaining a cool distance that was far from the emotional support she really needed.

'I take it you don't recognise it, then?'

'I've never seen it before. I mean, I know I must have done, but I don't remember any of it! I suppose we should take a look inside.'

But she couldn't bring herself to move. Number three, Norway Street was not a particularly attractive prospect, with its peeling paintwork and the decidedly grubby curtains in the windows. But it was more than that. Sitting here, looking across at the dilapidated house, Serena was suddenly a prey to a terrible sense of gloom, a feeling of dark apprehension as if something terrible was waiting for her behind that battered dark blue door.

'Would—would you come with me?'

'Sure. Just let me get Tonio.'

As she knocked uncertainly on the door, Serena found that

she was irrationally thankful that Tonio had been sound asleep in his special car seat when they had arrived and had stayed asleep when Rafael had transferred him to the comfort of his pushchair. Even though he wouldn't understand, probably wouldn't take in anything at all about his surroundings, she still felt happier that he wasn't really aware of them.

If she had lived here once, then she'd be willing to bet that she hadn't been dressed as she was now, she reflected edgily. Her clothes, though simply a casual beige trouser suit worn with a cream scoop neck tee shirt, declared their cost in their immaculate styling and superb fabric. It was the same with Rafael's navy polo shirt and matching chinos, with a loose, Italian-styled jacket on the top. The pair of them looked as out of place as a pair of peacocks in amongst a crowd of sparrows.

'Someone's coming.' Rafael spoke warningly just before the door was wrenched open.

'Yes?'

A hard-faced woman of around fifty with improbably blonde hair regarded them suspiciously from a dark and dingy hallway. Her eyes narrowed in swift appreciation as she took in Rafael's impressive height and strength, the tan obviously not acquired in England. But then her cold gaze went to Serena's face and the assessing stare was replaced by frank amazement.

'Well, well, well…if it isn't the mysterious Miss Martin finally turning up like a bad penny.'

'You—you know me?' Serena managed nervously.

'Know you! I should damn well think I do! And I'm not likely to forget you, am I, after you disappeared without a word—and owing me thr—?'

A hasty glance in Rafael's direction, a swift sizing up of the evident signs of wealth in his appearance, resulted in a rather obvious adjustment.

'Five months' rent.'

'Rent? I used to live here?'

'Back bedroom, first floor…' A jerk of the peroxide-bleached head indicated the position of the room before the woman realised just what Serena had said. 'What do you mean…?'

'Would it be possible to see the room, Mrs…' Rafael moved in to deflect the awkward questions it was clear she was about to ask.

'Potter. Marcia Potter. And, no, you can't see the room. I've let it out to someone else… Well, you'd vanished off the face of the earth,' she added sharply at Serena's cry of distress. 'I had no way of knowing if you were ever coming back, and you'd left me well out of pocket as it was.'

Rafael's sigh was a masterpiece of resignation and control.

'Five months' rent, I believe you said,' he inserted smoothly, stopping Serena's protest in its tracks with a distinctly warning glare. 'If we could just come inside then I'm sure we can sort this little matter out.'

'It may be a little matter to the likes of you…' Marcia Potter began indignantly, but the sight of Rafael's cheque-book as he took it from his inside pocket brought about another hasty readjustment. 'You'd best come in, then.'

The amount of rent quoted, considering the state of the house itself, made Serena gasp in horror, but Rafael appeared totally unperturbed as he began to write out a cheque.

'And Miss Martin can see the room,' he said, so easily that for a moment Marcia Potter didn't appreciate the unwavering determination behind the remark. But then she met the full cold force of those amber eyes as Rafael deliberately paused in what he was doing and made a move as if to put his pen away.

'Don't see no harm in it. After all, Mr Parkin is out at work at the moment. He works night shifts…'

'Back bedroom, first floor, I believe you said.' Rafael had no time for idle chat.

'That's right…' She pulled a bundle of keys from her pocket and selected one. 'Number four…'

It was worse than Serena could possibly have imagined. A cramped, miserable room with ugly floral wallpaper, faded and peeling, and stained vinyl flooring. A sagging, dirty-looking single bed stood against one wall, close to a cracked window, and a cheap melamine chest of drawers and a wardrobe were the only other furniture in the room.

Stunned into shocked silence, Serena could only stand in the doorway and stare, her hands coming up to cover her mouth and hold back the cry of horror that almost escaped her. Nausea roiled in her stomach, making her want to retch painfully.

How could she have endured living here for three seconds, let alone three months? And what had happened to her to reduce her to this level?

'Serena?'

Rafael's voice startled her out of her unhappy reverie. Lost in her unhappy thoughts, she hadn't heard him come up the stairs to join her.

'Do you—? *Madre de Dios*!'

If she had been shocked, then his reaction was hers multiplied a hundredfold. Which was not at all surprising, Serena reflected on a wave of bitterness. After all, Rafael Cordoba, international banker, the man who had homes in London, Almeria and Madrid, would never have seen anything like the sort of room that passed for accommodation at number three Norway Street, let alone have been forced to live in it.

'Come to see how the other half lives, eh, Rafael?' she challenged, too shocked by what she had seen and too disappointed by the total failure of the expedition to be able to control her response. 'Not exactly your luxurious multimillion-pound mansion, is it?'

'You lived *here*?'

'So it seems.'

Painfully aware of just how it must look through his eyes, she took refuge behind a shield of sharp flippancy, so as not to let him see the anguish that was eating away at her inside.

'This was my exclusive apartment—all mod cons, you see—with its beautiful decor, luxuriously appointed...'

'You remember it?' The question came swift as a striking snake and almost as deadly.

'Oh, come on, Rafael! You don't really expect me to answer that, do you?'

'Oh, but I do.' The four words were loaded with menace, making her stomach twist into tight, cruel knots of apprehension.

But, having started on this act to conceal her true misery, she couldn't just drop it now.

'How do you know you'll get an honest answer? After all, if I was to remember anything, then you would have fulfilled your responsibilities to me. You won't need to look after me any more and I'll be out on my ear, dropped right back into the world I came from. And who would want to come back to *this*?'

'I wouldn't do that to you.'

'No?'

Serena's smile was wide and brilliant, so brittle that she almost believed it would crack her lips.

'Of course you wouldn't. That's why you're my knight in shining armour, riding to my rescue in a very expensive car, bravely wielding your trusty chequebook!' The memory of that resigned sigh put an added edge to her words.

'*Serena!*'

She'd driven him too far. Flames blazed in the golden eyes, and his mouth was tight with fury.

'Do you or do you not remember anything about this hell-hole?'

'I... No,' Serena admitted despondently. 'No, I don't remember a thing. I suppose deep down I didn't really think I would, but I had to try.' A sudden thought struck her. 'Where's Tonio?'

'Downstairs.' Rafael's grimace was wry. 'Mrs Potter said

she'd keep an eye on him. Luckily he looked set to stay asleep for a while yet.'

'We'd better get back to him...'

She was moving out onto the dark landing as she spoke, but came to an abrupt halt as a strong hand clamped around her arm, holding her back.

'Serena, there is something you should know.'

Terrible images rushed into her head. A picture of Marcia Potter deciding to chat with Rafael while he had still been downstairs with her. Perhaps she had been able to enlighten him as to exactly what circumstances had brought Serena to live in this dump.

'What is it? *Rafael!*' she protested when he hesitated.

'Your clothes—and other bits and pieces. Mrs Potter sold most of them. She said she wanted to recoup some of the money you owed and so...'

'Oh, is that all?'

When she had expected something much more disturbing, something dreadful about her past, the sense of relief was like a rush of adrenaline to her brain, intoxicating her within seconds.

'Well, I won't worry about that! From the look of this place, any clothes I had back then would hardly be worth wearing. And I certainly don't need them now. I would probably just chuck them out anyway, seeing as I have a wonderful new wardrobe that you provided.'

No, that hadn't come out quite as she had meant it, and to judge by the sudden darkening of Rafael's eyes, the way his mouth suddenly thinned to a cruel, hard line, once again she'd overstepped some mark with him.

'I—I don't know how I'll ever be able to thank you!' she added hurriedly in an attempt to make up for her mistake.

'Don't you?'

The slow, dangerous smile told her exactly what was on his mind just before the hand that still held her jerked suddenly, pulling her hard up against the solid wall of his body.

'I think you know exactly how to show your gratitude,' he murmured smokily. 'But as that wouldn't be quite appropriate right now—I'll take this on account…'

His kiss was swift and hard, slightly cruel. He took her mouth with all the assurance of someone who was well aware of his rights and intended to assert them to the fullest. The caress had nothing of the tenderness, the seductive sensuality she had come to expect, and it left her feeling mentally bruised, suddenly shockingly vulnerable and disturbingly on the edge of tears.

'You can come up with the rest later—when we get back home.'

The words were like a slap in the face; all the warmth of that 'back home' was destroyed by the brutality of what had preceded it. It brought Serena up hard against a bitter truth that until now she had managed to avoid facing.

Over the past few days she had settled into Rafael's home as if she belonged there. She had loved being with him, loved looking after Tonio, loved the house, everything. But she'd been living in a fantasy world. She had actually come to see herself and Rafael as partners, taking care of his baby together. She had seen that arrangement stretching out into a future, seen herself by Rafael's side, being a mother to Tonio.

But Rafael had offered her nothing of the sort. He was quite content with the arrangement as it stood and had shown no sign of wanting anything more from it.

Somehow she dredged up enough strength to switch on that brilliant, fake smile once more.

'You better believe it!' she declared archly, but then a noise from down below caught her attention. 'Sounds like Tonio's stirring. I don't want him waking up and finding himself without the people he recognises.'

Grateful for the diversion, she hurried down the stairs, dropping down on her knees beside Tonio's pushchair as the little boy's eyes opened. The position gave her the chance to hide her face and the storm of emotion in her eyes from

Rafael, offering a few moments' breathing space to gather up the remnants of her composure and school her expression into something like calm.

'Hello, sweetie, did you have a good sleep? Rafael, I think we'd better get going. This little tyke is going to want feeding again before very long.'

They were on their way out of the door when Marcia Potter, who had vanished into one of the rooms off the hall, suddenly reappeared and caught hold of Serena's arm.

'You'd better have this...'

She pushed a large cardboard box forward until Serena had no choice but to take it.

'What is it?'

'Bits an' pieces you left behind. If you want them, of course, now that you've done so well for yourself.'

A nod of her bleached head indicated Rafael, who was now busily engaged in fastening the baby securely into his special car seat in spite of Tonio's loud protests at having been moved.

'Mrs Potter,' Serena said impulsively. 'When I was here— when I stayed with you—did I ever say anything—anything at all about my past? It's important!' she added urgently when the older woman looked at her suspiciously.

'Well, you weren't exactly the chatty type. And you know me; I don't like to pry into my lodgers' business. But you did mention you came from Yorkshire, and that you were down on your luck.'

One thing she already knew, and the other anyone could have guessed from the simple fact that she had stayed here. Serena bit down hard on her lower lip to keep back the moan of disappointment.

'Must admit I never put much faith in your rich Spaniard, but it seems you landed on your feet right enough.'

'What?' Serena frowned in shocked confusion. 'I don't understand.'

'I was sure you wouldn't see him for dust, but you had

stars in your eyes and were convinced he'd stand by you. Just goes to show…'

'Serena!'

Rafael's call cut into their conversation, clear and autocratic and just impatient enough to make it plain that he was none too pleased at having to hang around.

'If we don't get back soon it'll be way past Tonio's meal time and he'll start screaming the place down.'

'I'd get off, if I were you,' Marcia Potter advised matter-of-factly. 'Doesn't look like the sort of man who likes to be kept waiting, your feller. You don't want to push him too far; I'd bet he can be pretty scary in a temper.'

'You can say that again,' Serena began, but broke off as another roar from Rafael, his temper obviously shifting up a notch, demanded her attention. 'I'm coming!' she said in a hasty attempt to pacify him. 'Honest! It's just…'

But when she turned back to Marcia, the other woman was no longer there. She had gone back indoors, the door swinging shut with a bang that made it plain their conversation was at an end.

'Serena!'

It was clear that Rafael wouldn't tolerate any further delay. Already he was revving the engine with a fierce, angry sound that had her dashing to the car and jumping into her seat in a rush, fearful that he might actually drive off and leave her there.

'What kept you?' he demanded when Norway Street had been left well behind and they were heading back to his house, travelling at a speed that Serena was convinced had more to do with his state of mind than any urgency about Tonio's next bottle. 'I wouldn't have thought you'd have much to chat to Mrs Potter about.'

'If you must know, I asked her if I'd told her anything about myself while I was there. Do you have to drive this fast?' she demanded in sharp reproof as the engine roared again. 'We do have a baby in the back!'

'I'm well aware of Tonio's presence!' Rafael tossed at her, the muscles in his mouth and jaw clenched tight over some strong emotion. 'And I am totally in control.'

'I'm sure you are—of the car at least! I just wish I could say the same of your temper. Slow down!'

Rafael's only response was a low growl of anger, but Serena was thankful to see that he did ease up on the accelerator and they continued at a much more sedate pace.

'Thank you!' she said primly, expecting, and getting, a glare in response, but one that, she was glad to see, was only really half serious.

'You didn't get anything new out of Señora Potter,' he said abruptly, and it was couple of seconds before Serena realised that his words had been a statement, not a question. 'I'd already grilled her about you,' he elucidated when she turned a puzzled face to him.

'You might have told me that!'

The shrug that lifted the broad shoulders under the navy jacket was supremely indifferent to her indignation.

'It wasn't important. She had nothing to say that was of any use.'

Except a mention of a rich Spaniard, Serena recalled uneasily, knowing she wasn't yet ready to talk about her former landlady's mysterious comment, if she would ever be. Just what had Marcia meant about her 'rich Spaniard'? She couldn't possibly have been talking about Rafael because he had been in Almeria all the time Serena had lived in Norway Street.

Or had he? He had said he'd been in Spain when the accident had occurred, but he'd never mentioned any time before that. Was the possibility of *two* rich Spaniards being involved in her life just too coincidental to be possible?

Suddenly she felt desperately cold, in spite of the warmth of the sun through the car window,

'What's in the box?' Rafael was unaware of her uncomfortable change of mood.

'Bits and pieces... Things I left behind in my room.'

'Things Ma Potter didn't think were worth selling,' Rafael returned cynically. 'Anything that's any help?'

'I don't know.'

Had his tone changed suddenly, or was it just her imagination? Serena shifted uneasily in her seat. She didn't like the way she was beginning to feel, the suspicions that kept sliding into her mind. She should just ask him straight out, but she knew she didn't dare. She was just too terrified to consider the possible implications for her own future if she found out something she didn't want to know.

'I haven't looked.'

'Well, don't you think it's time you did?'

Serena tugged at the tight-fitting lid of the box, feeling as nervous as if she had been told there was an angry cobra inside, just waiting to strike.

'There's a passport,' she told him, rooting through the meagre contents. 'A few photos of my mum and dad—and here's one of me with Leanne! A building society book—address Ryeton, of course—and the vast sum of twenty pounds to my name. Oh, but this is more like it...'

She brandished a small red-backed notebook.

'What's that?'

He sounded supremely casual, his attention apparently on the roundabout he was negotiating. Surely she was just imagining things? He couldn't have anything to hide, could he?

'It's my address book. At least this way I'll be able to get in touch with Leanne if nothing else.'

'Anyone else listed in there who might help?'

'Nope. I remember all these people, so they must be from the time before I lost my memory.'

They had reached the gates to Rafael's house now, and so she dropped the address book back into the box with a thud and replaced the lid.

'What time will it be in Sydney right now?'

'Let me see—about three in the morning. Definitely not a good time to ring Leanne, if that's what you were thinking.'

'You're right.' Reluctantly Serena let go of the idea of doing just that. 'But perhaps by the time I've got Tonio fed, bathed and into bed...'

'A much more sensible idea.' Rafael brought the big car to a smooth halt outside the front door. 'Why don't you go and sort out the bottle while I bring his lordship in?'

As always, the bustle and fun of feeding, bathing and settling Tonio for the night lifted Serena's mood and pushed some of her earlier disappointment and unease from her thoughts. The cardboard box was dumped in her bedroom and temporarily forgotten about, and it wasn't until she went to change after Tonio's enthusiastic splashings had soaked her through that she remembered it again.

Pausing in the act of peeling off her wet tee shirt, she checked her watch hastily. Still only eight. That meant it would be much too early in Australia. She'd have to wait another couple of hours at least.

Dropping the tee shirt on the floor, she opened the box and pulled out the address book once more. As she flicked through it, finding Leanne's address, a small piece of paper, unnoticed before, fell out and landed on the carpet. Bending down hastily, Serena picked it up, then froze as she saw what was written on it.

The note was brief, only one word and a string of numbers, but the impact it had, stabbing straight to her heart like a brutal stiletto, was totally out of proportion to its size. It made her head reel, her breath still. Every trace of colour leached from her face, and a low, agonised moan of disbelief escaped her ashen lips.

Cordoba, it read, in handwriting that she knew was her own. And the string of numbers that followed was nothing less than the telephone number, complete with dialing code, of the house she was now in—Rafael's house.

CHAPTER ELEVEN

'SERENA?'

Rafael's voice startled her out of her shocked trance, her coppery head coming up sharply as she looked round for somewhere to hide the note with its disturbing information. She couldn't tackle him about it until she'd had time to think about what it might mean to her.

Not the box Marcia had given her. Rafael might want to look through that again. And she was too far from her chest of drawers...

Already the door was opening. The note was still in her hand. In a rush of desperation she pushed it into her trouser pocket, crumpling it badly.

'Serena...?'

Spinning round, she faced him wide-eyed and breathing rapidly. She was just in time to catch the alteration in his expression, the move from slightly annoyed enquiry to dark-eyed sensual appreciation in the blink of one thickly lashed eye. His survey was a caress in itself as it slid from her flushed face, down over the exposed skin of her chest and shoulder to the creamy curves of her breasts exposed by the white lace of her bra.

'That's what I like to see,' he drawled indolently. 'A woman who does half the work for me.'

With an effort Serena resisted the impulse to fold her arms around her body, hiding herself from that insolently appraising dark gaze. Painfully aware of the incriminating piece of paper hidden in her pocket, she didn't think before launching herself into the attack.

'Don't you ever knock?'

Black straight brows arched upwards at her outburst.

139

'Was I supposed to? I thought we were way past that. And besides, I thought we had an arrangement.'

'Arrangement? What arrangement?'

But even as she spoke she knew.

I don't know how I'll ever be able to thank you, she had said. And he had made it so very plain that there was one very easy way to express her gratitude.

'What is it, *querida*?' Rafael enquired sardonically as she hesitated. 'Not so grateful after all?'

'On the contrary,' Serena managed honestly. 'After what I saw this afternoon, I'm more grateful to you than ever. When I think of what you rescued me from, what I might have had to go back to...'

Recalling the sordid ugliness of Norway Street, she couldn't hold back on a shudder of distaste.

'I can't tell you what it means to me.'

'Then show me...'

One long hand came out in that imperious gesture she knew so well, motioning to her to come to him. And yet somehow this time there seemed to be something else behind it. A new tension in the strong body. An expression she couldn't read in the watchful golden eyes.

'Show me, Serena. Show me how grateful you are. Show me what is in your heart...'

Show me what is in your heart. If only she could. If only she dared.

No. She quailed away from it even in the same moment that a tiny quiver of hope twisted deep inside her. How could she expose herself so completely to him when he had spoken no word of love or shown any sign of wanting anything more than the relationship they already had?

And yet how could she not? How could she stay silent for ever on something that mattered so much to her? How long could she hide her feelings from him? For the rest of her life?

Someone had to make the first move. Someone had to take

the risk of opening their heart without the certainty that their feelings were returned.

And suddenly it was shockingly simple. It was disturbingly, almost frighteningly easy. All she had to do was to step forward and lift her arms, entwining them around his neck, drawing that arrogant head slowly down towards hers, brushing the sensual mouth with her own.

'I'll show you,' she whispered. 'I'll show you what it means—how I feel...'

She didn't get a chance to say another word as his mouth closed over hers, taking the kiss she offered and returning it with an intensity that turned the mood from anticipation to burning passion in the space of a single heartbeat.

If she had thought that she'd seen him hungry before, it had been as nothing when compared with the urgency of his demands now. It was as if she had opened a floodgate and found herself submerged in the resulting torrent that poured out, swirling around her, swamping her, making her gasp for breath.

His sigh against her mouth was raw and unsteady, his eyes tightly closed as if to hide their secrets from her. It was his hands and his lips that communicated his need without words.

One arm slid behind her shoulders, the other curving around her waist, and the next moment she was lifted from the floor and carried over to the bed, where he lowered her onto the soft turquoise and white quilt, coming down beside her in the space of a single breath.

And now he did open his eyes. And, looking up into them, Serena saw that they were pitch-black, no trace of any corona of colour, just the deepest, darkest pools that seemed to draw her into them, as if into his soul.

'Serena, *mi encantadora*,' he muttered thickly, sliding the satin straps of her bra down her arms to expose the soft swell of her breasts. 'You are so beautiful, how could any man resist you?'

Her smile in response was slightly tremulous, fraying at the edges, her big brown eyes misting with tears.

'Then don't try,' she whispered back. 'Don't—!'

The words broke off on a cry of delight as his mouth found her breast and all rational thought vanished in the second that its moist warmth closed over one aching nipple. It took only a couple of seconds of Rafael's sure, knowing caresses, a string of those heated kisses, to wipe all the careful reasoning, all the newly acknowledged hope and dreams from her mind.

She didn't care what Rafael's feelings for her were. They no longer mattered. He had said she was lovely—beautiful—irresistible—and for now that was enough. If he couldn't resist her, he would stay with her, and that was all that she needed for now.

And as Rafael's strong body merged with hers she found that her own emotions overwhelmed her, making her cry out loud. Convulsively she arched her back so that she was as close to him as she could be, as if their two bodies could fuse together at mouth and breast and hip, as well as at that most intimate joining of all.

She stayed like that, open to him, yearning against him, until the climax took her, flinging her over the edge into a whirlpool of sensation that was like the buffeting of the wildest tropical storm.

She didn't know how long it took her to come back to reality, or how long he had lain there watching her. She only knew that when her heavy eyelids struggled open Rafael was stretched out at her side, propped up on one elbow, his head resting on his hand, heavy lids hooding his eyes.

'Why are you crying?' he asked softly when he saw her brown gaze turn to him.

'I…' Serena frowned uncertainly. 'I'm not.'

'No?'

With the lightest touch imaginable he reached out his free hand and traced the soft skin under her eyes. To her consternation Serena could feel the damp trail of tears along the path of his fingertips, and when she brought her own hands up, rubbing the backs of them along her cheeks, they came away revealingly wet.

'I didn't know...'

Struggling to sit up, she raised herself a little against the downy pillows, then froze, transfixed, as those heavy lids lifted and the golden eyes blazed straight into hers.

'You didn't know...' he echoed huskily. 'Which makes me all the more curious as to *why*? Why the tears, *querida*? Why should our lovemaking make you weep?'

'Because...'

She hunted for words, for some sort of explanation, and nothing would come to mind. Nothing, that was, apart from the absolute truth.

'Because it was so wonderful. So beautiful. Because you are so beautiful.'

'Beautiful?' She'd surprised him now, his proud head going back in shock. 'Serena...'

'Oh, I know!' Laughter bubbled up inside her at the look on his face. 'Beautiful isn't the word you'd expect me to use to describe a man, is it? But it's the only word I want to use to describe you. Because to me you are beautiful—because I—I love you!'

There, now it was out, and she was glad she'd said it. She didn't regret it, or wish a single word back because it was the absolute truth and she could no longer hide it from him, no longer keep it to herself.

But then she looked up into his strongly carved face, the handsome features shadowed by the gathering darkness, and her heart clenched painfully in fear. The relaxed warmth, the gentleness of just moments before had vanished, and his expression was as cold and distant as if steel shutters had just come down behind his eyes, cutting him off from her.

'Madre de Dios!'

Cursing savagely in Spanish, he jack-knifed his long body

up and off the bed, snatching up his discarded clothes and
pulling them on with rough, angry movements that spoke
eloquently of his total withdrawal from her, the total loss of
the closeness they had shared such a short time before.

'Rafael…'

Too shocked and distressed to form any other words, she
could only use his name to plead with him to turn to her, to
explain why he had reacted so violently. But her appeal
seemed to bounce off the strong, hard line of his back, his
stiffly held spine, as he stamped his feet into his shoes with
a force that made her wonder if he wished he had her awkward heart and its inconvenient feelings beneath the fine
hand-stitched leather soles.

'Rafael… Please…'

Now he did turn round, but when she saw his face she
could only wish that he hadn't. If there had been rejection in
his stance, in the way he had turned away from her, it was
there in spades in his expression. She had never seen him
look so icily remote, so blackly hostile. His stunning features
might have been carved out of granite for all the emotion,
all the warmth she could see there.

'*Love.*' He almost spat the word out as if it was a savage
curse. 'Serena, do not say such a thing, even as a joke.'

'A *joke!*'

She couldn't believe what she was hearing.

'I wasn't making a joke! I was deadly serious! I meant
what I said, Rafael! I… I…'

But she couldn't say the words again, not with those cold
golden eyes burning into her, the eyes of a hunter, of a soar-
ing golden eagle, looking for its prey.

She had seen that arrogantly dismissive flick of his hand
so many times, but never had it seemed quite so autocratic,
quite so stamped with rejection of all she was saying.

'You cannot love me because you do not know me. You
cannot claim to know anyone as long as you have this memory loss—this missing year. You—'

'But don't you see? That's just the point! When I'm with you that missing year just ceases to matter. I don't care about it, in fact I don't really mind if it never comes back, because with you I have something to put in its place!'

'*Maldito sea!* Do not say that! You can't put me in the place of that lost life! I'm not free to be anything to you. I do not *want* to be anything to you.'

Feeling the harsh words like blows to her heart, Serena shrank back against the pillows, painfully conscious of her vulnerable nakedness while he was so strongly armoured by being fully dressed. Her clouded brown eyes went to where her clothes lay scattered on the floor; she wished she could find the strength to move to gather them up. Even if she couldn't put them on, at least she could hold them against her as some form of protection.

Her clothes. Her mind seemed to blow a fuse as the sight of her crumpled trousers brought back in a rush the memory of the moment when Rafael had walked through the door; the piece of paper she had hastily shoved into her pocket. The note that seemed to indicate Rafael was not telling the truth about whether he had known her before.

'H-how do you feel about me?' She had to struggle to force the words past lips that seemed to have frozen in the ice of his glare.

'Feel?'

He looked stunned that she should even ask the question, shocked to even have to consider it.

'You know how I feel. I want you—you're one very sexy lady. I only have to look at you to feel aroused—to feel hunger for you. And that hunger shows no sign of abating, no matter how many times we sleep together. But I sure as hell don't love you.'

'You don't?'

What sort of fool was she? A masochist of the first order? She'd heard what he'd said, hadn't she? Did she truly want him to confirm his lack of feeling for her? Why not just offer him the chance to tear her heart out of her chest and toss it carelessly aside? The effect would be much the same.

'Serena.' Rafael's tone was huskily vehement, his accent strongly marked. 'Have I ever misled you—ever offered you anything more than what we already have? Have I ever promised you love and a future and happy ever after?'

'N-no.'

'No. And that is because I cannot deliver. I never make promises I cannot keep, and I don't intend to start now. If you're looking for that sort of reassurance, then you have the wrong man.'

'I think you're right.'

Her voice was low and flat, completely lifeless, reflecting the state of her heart. In her mind she could hear Rafael's voice, hear once again the promise he had made her in the car on the way to his house from the hospital.

I can promise you that as long as you are in my home, under my protection, I will ensure that you do not hurt anyone, in any way, as a consequence of the things you do not remember, he had said. But he hadn't been able to promise that she wouldn't hurt *herself.*

And she was hurting now. Hurting cruelly, savagely, so that she wanted to curl up into a little ball and fold her arms around herself, to try to hold together a spirit that seemed to be shattering into tiny, irreparable pieces inside her.

But she could never do that while Rafael was still in the room.

'I'd like you to leave now,' she managed stiffly.

'Serena?'

But she couldn't take any more.

'Just go!' she slung at him. 'Go—get out of my room and leave me alone!'

She had thought she had already known the depths of unhappiness, but that was before she saw the silent, stiff little inclination of his head that was his only acknowledgement, the way he turned and marched out of the room without a

single glance back. It was only then that she really scraped
the bottom of the barrel of misery, hot, bitter tears welling
up in her eyes, stinging cruelly. And as Rafael closed the
door firmly behind him she finally gave in to them and let
them flow.

Serena had no idea at exactly what point sleep had claimed
her. She only knew that at some time, late into the night,
exhaustion and despair had finally overwhelmed her and she
had fallen into a shallow and uneasy doze. By that moment
her misery had been worsened even further by her vain attempts to contact Leanne in Australia. The impersonal, au-
tomated tones of a telephone answering machine had been
the only response to her call, and she had been forced to
leave a message asking her friend to call her back instead of
indulging in the long, informative talk she had hoped for.

And even the sleep she'd managed hadn't been the peace-
ful oblivion she needed. Instead she had been plunged into
a dark and frightening morass of images and scenes that
made no sense. In her dreams distress piled on fear, adding
horror onto horror, until at last she had wrenched herself
awake, lying shaking and sweating, her heart pounding with
remembered panic.

Tonio. The first rational thought that penetrated the fog of
fear that clouded her mind was for the baby. She suddenly
had the most terrible sense of dread, the impression that
something was appallingly wrong with the little boy. That he
needed her. That he was crying out to her...

It was only when she skidded into the baby's bedroom,
not even having stopped to pick up her robe in her headlong
flight, that she realised her mistake. The fear, the sense of
horror, had not been real, but the lingering after-effects of
her nightmare, clinging like sticky, dust-covered cobwebs to
the half-awake surface of her mind.

'Tonio...'

His name escaped her on a sigh as she sank down on the

carpeted floor beside his cot, resting her head against its wooden frame, watching the small boy sleeping soundly. With one shaking finger she gently smoothed the soft black hair on his tiny head, her pulse-rate slowly easing from its frantic race as a degree of calm returned.

She hadn't been dreaming about Tonio, she remembered. Now she vividly remembered exactly what her dream had been about. And the reason why she had dreamed it was here in her hand. The piece of paper with Rafael's phone number on it. She had pulled it from her pocket last thing, held it like a talisman, and she had fallen asleep still clutching it.

As a result she had fallen back into the dream she had had on her first night in this house. The dream about the car. The darkness. The noise. The screams. The dream where, last time, she had thought that Rafael had been there with her.

And now she knew exactly why she had thought that. Now, with the memory of her nightmare clear in her mind, she could recall just what had made her thoughts jump straight to Rafael as soon as she had woken. The dark, masculine figure in her dream had been only a vague shape, no features clearly defined, but she had heard his voice only too clearly.

The angry, cruel words he had flung at her were fading now, but there was no mistaking the accent that had shaded every sound. The *Spanish* accent. The same accent she heard every time Rafael spoke.

Must admit I never put much faith in your rich Spaniard. Marcia Potter's words came back to haunt her, as did the memory of the note she had found in her address book. The telephone number that could be no one's but Rafael's.

'Oh, God!'

It was a low moan of despair as she faced the reality she had tried to avoid for so long.

She had trusted Rafael, put her life into his hands. She had even given him her heart, falling blindly, foolishly, irredeemably in love with a man she didn't even know. A man who, by his own admission, didn't love her.

And now, it seemed, a man who had lied to her all along.

She couldn't stay here.

The resolve came swift and hard on the heels of the reeling sense of shock. She couldn't continue to live in this house, sleep in the same bed, *make love* with a man who had abused her trust, her naïvety, her *heart* so appallingly. She couldn't stay here another minute. She would…

But if she walked out on Rafael then that would also mean leaving Tonio behind.

Immediately Serena's resolve faded as rapidly as it had come, all the strength seeping from her like the air from a punctured balloon.

Tonio. How could she ever leave the little boy who had captured her heart every bit as strongly as his father?

'Oh, I can't!' She couldn't hold the words back, even though she knew Tonio, still fast asleep, couldn't hear them. 'I can't! I *can't!*'

'You can't what?'

Rafael's voice was low, pitched so as not to wake the sleeping baby, but it still came with such force, so totally unexpected, that Serena leapt like a scalded cat, spinning round on her knees to face him as he stood in the doorway.

Unlike her, hearing the sound of her movements, he had paused to pull on some clothes. Either that or he had never been to bed at all. It was more likely the latter, Serena thought, registering the fact that the navy polo shirt and trousers were the same garments he had flung on in a fury at her foolishly precipitate declaration of love. His eyes looked heavy too, with smudges of shadow dimming their gold to cloudy amber.

'I—I didn't know you were there!'

'Obviously, or you would not have been so open in your admission of your feelings, I presume? But I was here, and you did express those feelings—so now are you going to tell me exactly what you meant?'

He might have couched the words in the form of a question, but only a fool would have had any doubt that they were actually a command. And a command he fully intended to have obeyed.

There was also no way he would be satisfied with anything other than the truth, Serena realised. Looking up into the fierce golden gaze that made her feel uncomfortably like some delicate butterfly, pinned out on a laboratory slide, ready to be examined under a microscope, she knew there was no way she could dodge the issue.

Besides, she felt too emotionally battered, too worn down by the night's events, not least by the terror of her dreams, to have the mental strength to even try and come up with a believable story.

'I can't leave Tonio,' she told him, lifting her chin with a touch of defiance and meeting his hard stare head-on, even though she had to throw back her head in order to do so. 'I love him so much—he's stolen my heart and I don't want it to be let go. But as a result I just can't leave him, no matter what happens.'

Tonio and his father, she admitted to herself in the privacy of her own thoughts. No matter what had happened, in spite of the blunt cruelty of his rejection, his forceful declaration that he felt no love for her, she still couldn't turn and walk away from Rafael. Not without shattering her heart completely.

'And why would you have to leave him?' He was the Spanish Inquisitor once again, but this time with a deadly softness to the question that was more terrifying than the sternly rapped out interrogations he had subjected her to before.

'You know why!'

She regretted the sharpness of her voice as soon as she had spoken, her eyes going swiftly to the cot to check that she hadn't disturbed the sleeping child. But Tonio simply stirred slightly, murmuring faintly in his sleep, then resumed his deep, regular breathing.

'I had that dream again tonight,' she continued in a quieter tone. 'The one when I'm in the car.'

Something in her tone, in her expression obviously struck home. The shadowed eyes narrowed swiftly, the sensual mouth tightening, his jaw setting hard.

'We will talk about this outside,' he declared grimly, holding out one hand with the obvious intention of helping her to her feet.

For a couple of seconds Serena was tempted to ignore both the gesture and the immediate obedience he expected, but another soft sound from Tonio changed her mind. They could hardly have this out in this room without waking him.

Steeling herself against the immediate electric reaction of every nerve in her body at the feel of his flesh against hers, she took hold of Rafael's proffered hand and allowed herself to be eased upright, but then found that once he had her fingers prisoner Rafael simply refused to let go.

'Rafael!' she whispered in a furious undertone.

But that too was ignored, and, forced either to quicken her steps to match his forceful stride or to be dragged ignominiously along in his wake, she was swept out of Tonio's room and into the one next door. Rafael's bedroom.

'I don't want to talk in here...' she began protestingly, unable even to look in the direction of the big double bed where she and Rafael had spent so many long, sensual nights.

'Where we talk is irrelevant. It is what we talk about that matters,' Rafael retorted, snapping on the light with a suddenness that made Serena jump violently, blinking hard as she adjusted to the unaccustomed brilliance. 'So now,' he continued, rounding on her dangerously, 'you will tell me why you were thinking of leaving.'

'Isn't it obvious?'

The fact that he needed to ask was like another knife in

her heart. Did he really think that she would just swallow down his assertion that he didn't love her and let their relationship continue on a level of pure sex and nothing more?

'The dream.'

The look he turned on her was starkly disbelieving, blazing with contempt.

'So because of a night-time fantasy, you are prepared to pack up—'

'It isn't just a night-time fantasy, and you know it!' Serena cut in on him frantically, desperate to convince him. 'It's much more than that. It's a link to my past...'

'You imagine.'

'I *know*. Rafael, I've had this dream before, remember, and you said the car I described was the right one. And tonight I was closer, so much closer to remembering.'

She had his attention now. The curtly dismissive attitude had vanished, replaced by a fierce-eyed attention that made her swallow nervously before she could go on.

'I heard the driver's voice. He spoke to me just before I screamed...'

'So now I suppose you are going to accuse me of being the driver...'

'Well, weren't you? I want the truth this time, Rafael— the real, honest truth! I don't want you fobbing me off with stories of another driver. Who? Your chauffeur, perhaps—a chauffeur with a Spanish accent identical to yours. I want to know where I was going, and who with, and...'

Suddenly she realised that ever since she had woken, throughout the time she had spent in Tonio's room, she had still had the note she had found in her address book clutched in her hand, where it had been since she had woken up.

'And I want you to explain this!'

With a wild gesture she flung the paper straight into Rafael's face. He watched impassively as it fluttered to the ground, then stooped with lithe grace to pick it up. She saw his expression change dramatically as he read what was on it, lines of strain suddenly etched around his aristocratic nose and mouth.

'Where did you find this?'

'In my address book. The one that Marcia Potter had all this time in Norway Street. That's my handwriting, Rafael. My handwriting and your phone number, which proves that I knew about you before you ever visited me in that hospital. So now tell me the truth about this other driver—'

'No estaba el chófer!' Rafael broke in on her suddenly, his voice raw and uneven, his superb knowledge of English deserting him in the force of his emotions. *'Estaba mi hermano!'*

'What?'

Serena could only stare in blank confusion, shocked by the violence of his tone, not knowing the reasons behind it.

'Rafael, I don't understand.'

Rafael drew in a deep, ragged sigh as he raked both hands through the ebony silk of his hair, obviously struggling for control.

'The driver was not the chauffeur,' he translated with obvious reluctance, his eyes shockingly black with pain. 'He was my brother.'

CHAPTER TWELVE

As SOON as Rafael brought the car to a halt at the front of the house, Serena pushed her door open and got out hurriedly, unable to bear being close to him any longer. The past few days had been the worst sort of strain, the long journey today hell on earth. And it had all been such a total waste of time.

When Rafael had suggested that they travel to Yorkshire, visit the places she could remember, go back to the time before her memory had been destroyed, she had jumped at the chance. She would have done anything at all if it only offered her the possibility of some sort of explanation of what had happened, and, more importantly, why she had behaved as she had.

Even now, five days later, she still found it hard to take in just what Rafael had told her.

'The driver was not the chauffeur,' he had said in that nightmare moment in the early dawn. 'He was my brother.'

'Your...' She had to struggle to force the words out. 'I didn't even know you had a brother!'

'My younger brother,' Rafael had flung into her white, shocked face. 'I am—I was—five years older.'

And then he had added the final, even more shocking words, that had sent her spinning into a world of dark confusion where nothing she had ever believed about herself seemed to hold true.

'You and Felipe were lovers.'

'You look worn out.' Rafael came up behind her now, the handles of Tonio's carrycot held in one strong, brown hand. 'Why don't you go straight to bed? I'll see to the baby.'

'No!' Serena rejected the idea with a vehement shake of her bright head.

If she went to bed, she wouldn't sleep. Instead she would lie awake, as she had done every night since she had learned the truth, staring at the ceiling, trying to work out just how she could forget a man who had been her lover—for almost a year, it seemed.

'I'll do it. You have the cases to bring in.'

And keeping busy with Tonio would mean she didn't have to spend yet more awkward, stiffly uncomfortable time in Rafael's company. Her nerves felt stretched until they were at breaking point and it was as if some vital protective layer of skin had been slowly scraped away, leaving her agonisingly raw and vulnerable. She desperately needed a break, some time to herself.

'All right,' Rafael conceded with the same careful politeness as he had used towards her ever since he had suggested the trip to Yorkshire. 'I'll put your bag in your room.'

Serena could only nod silently, taking Tonio from him and hurrying inside before he could detect just how close to tears she was.

Your room. If anything revealed the distance that had come between them, it was this. For their stay in the North Rafael had booked separate rooms in each hotel they had stayed in. And he had kept very firmly to his own domain, leaving her completely alone in hers.

She dragged out the task of settling Tonio for the night as long as she could though really there was not much involved in it. Because of the lateness of the hour, the little boy was already out for the count, barely stirring when she changed his nappy and laid him in his cot. But then she had to decide what to do with what remained of the evening.

'Serena!' Rafael called up to her from the hallway. 'I've made some coffee. If Tonio's settled, I'm sure you could do with a drink.'

And she was sure that it would choke her if she tried to

swallow anything. But she strongly suspected that if she lingered upstairs any longer Rafael was capable of coming to get her, marching her down to the sitting room by force if necessary.

So she contented herself with spending a little more time freshening up in the *en suite* bathroom to her room, splashing water on her face in a vain effort to bring a little more colour to her cheeks and running a brush through her hair. Then, knowing she was already pushing Rafael as far as she could, she smoothed down the moss-green linen trousers she wore with a scoop-necked toning stretch cotton top, drew in a deep breath and headed downstairs.

'There are some sandwiches as well.'

Rafael's tone was carefully matter of fact. If he noticed the shadows under her dark eyes, the defiant set of her head, he made no comment, but simply gestured towards the coffee table and the laden tray that stood on it.

'I'm not hungry.'

'But you ate nothing on the journey. You—'

'Rafael, I said I'm not hungry! I'm not Tonio—you don't have to watch over me to make sure I eat enough.'

'Caring for Tonio is simple compared to managing you!' Rafael muttered darkly, his anger revealed in the betraying thickening of his accent until the words were almost unintelligible. 'Serena, I know that the past few days have been difficult...'

'Difficult!' Serena echoed with cynical satire. 'I think that's something of an understatement. I started out with a black hole where the past year should be, then discovered that for twelve months or so I'd had a Spanish lover—a man whose name I wouldn't even remember if you hadn't told me it. A man whose face would be just a blank if you hadn't produced those photographs!'

Her voice shook tremulously on the last sentence as she recalled the sheer horror of being shown a picture that Rafael assured her was of his brother, Felipe. She had stared down into the face of a man whose only claim to looking at all familiar was his similarity to Rafael himself, and had felt as if the world had come crashing down on her, obliterating everything she had believed was true.

'A man you say was my lover and yet I have no recollection of ever being with him...'

But she could remember Rafael's lovemaking.

Oh, God, she could still feel the imprint of his hands, his kisses, as if they were branded into her flesh. She had no doubt at all that now Rafael had made love to her that it would take more than a blow on the head to wipe that memory from her mind.

'And now we've spent the past five days wandering round Yorkshire, trailing here, there and everywhere, looking for my past, for some clue to where I met this man, how I met him... And have come back with what?' Her voice cracked, breaking in the middle as she fought back tears of savage disappointment. 'Precisely nothing!'

But at least Rafael had tried; she had to grant him that. Seeing her panic and distress, the shocking effect that the revelations about her relationship with Felipe had had on her, he had come up with the idea of the trip to Yorkshire in the hope that visiting some of her old haunts would somehow jog her memory, bring something back to her. It wasn't his fault that the whole expedition had been a total disaster.

'But still I ought to thank you for trying. It was kind...'

'Kind!' The word was a sound of exasperation, of disbelief. 'I did not do this to be kind! I—'

He broke off with a violent curse as the sound of the telephone shrilled out in the hall, startling them both.

'Leave it!' he commanded as Serena turned automatically to answer its summons.

'I can't—it might wake Tonio.'

Besides which, she needed a moment or two out of the room. A little time away from Rafael's overwhelming physical presence. Time to draw breath, collect her scattered thoughts, try to drag her whirling emotions back under some degree of control.

'Hello?' In spite of all her efforts, her voice squeaked embarrassingly as she spoke into the receiver.

'Serena?' A laughing female voice answered her. 'Is that you? You sound so strange.'

'I'm sorry, do...?' But then realisation dawned in a rush of delighted relief. 'Lee? Leanne—it is Leanne, isn't it?'

'Of course it's me!' her friend declared, her voice so clear that she might have been phoning from next door rather than the other side of the world. 'You left a message on the answering machine asking me to ring you as soon as I got back. I'm sorry it's taken so long, but we've been away. But what about you? I take it that since you gave me this number you and Felipe are back together again?'

Felipe. Shock made Serena's mind reel so sickeningly that she had to reach out and grasp a nearby chair for support.

'Did you say Felipe? You *know* about him?'

'Of course I know about him.' There was no mistaking Leanne's confusion. 'Serena, is there something wrong? I thought you said this was the Cordoba number, so naturally I assumed...'

'It *is* the Cordoba house, but—but it's not *Felipe's* house. It's Rafael's...'

As she spoke, Serena was painfully conscious of the door that still stood open behind her. Out of the corner of her eye she could just see how Rafael, who had been pacing around the sitting room like some restless, caged jungle cat, had now come to a complete halt and was listening to her half of the conversation in the sort of frozen stillness that made all the tiny hairs on the back of her neck lift in shivering tension.

'Rafael?' At the other end of the telephone line Leanne echoed the name in a voice that increased Serena's inner tension one thousandfold. 'Is big brother Rafael there? Oh, Lord, Serena, sweetie! What sort of mess has Felipe got himself into now?'

The buzzing sound inside Serena's head was like that of hundreds of angry bees, making her feel as if she was about to faint. Weakly she sank down into the chair, her legs refusing to support her any longer.

'I—I suppose you could say the worst sort of mess possible,' she managed unevenly. 'Lee, there was an accident…Felipe's dead.'

The word fell into the sort of shocked silence that reverberated furiously round and round in her skull. It took Leanne several attempts to speak, and when she did her voice had lost all the light and laughter that had been in it before.

'Dead?' she echoed disbelievingly. 'Oh, Serena…! No wonder big brother's turned up, then. Naturally he'd be the one to sort things out. But what about you—and Tonio—how's little Tonio?'

'Tonio? How…?'

As she struggled to speak, a movement in the sitting room caught her eye. Rafael had taken a single step forward, then stopped, his hands coming up in a gesture that Serena could only interpret as one of resignation. But, having glanced his way, she found she couldn't look away again. The golden blaze of his eyes locked with her own wide brown ones, holding her bewildered gaze with a mesmeric force as she struggled to continue her conversation.

'How do you know about Tonio? I mean—naturally he's here with his father.'

'His father?' If Leanne had sounded shocked before, now she sounded positively dazed, as if her sense of reality had been totally shattered. 'Serena—are you all right? I mean, you just said…'

'I should have explained.' Serena found she was gabbling the words out, her own already shaky mood affected by her friend's reaction. 'When I said there had been an accident—it was a car crash. I was in the car too and I hit my head. Lee—I feel like my mind's been scrambled. There are so many things I can't remember. The past year and everything

that happened in it has gone completely. If there's anything
you can tell me— anything at all…'

At the other end of the telephone line Leanne drew in a
long, deep breath then let it out again in a rush, the sound
taking Serena's tension up several agonising notches.

'The past year? And you remember absolutely nothing?
Then Serena, my love, there's something absolutely vital that
you should know. And for some reason it looks like I'm
going to have to be the one to tell you.'

Serena had no idea whether she sat there, the receiver
glued to her ear, for five, ten, or even twenty minutes. She
only knew that she couldn't have moved if she'd tried. That
all her control over her limbs, all her ability to think, had
abandoned her. She could only manage to stay upright by
sheer force of will.

And all the time her bruised, darkened gaze was locked
with Rafael's, unable to look away, unable even to blink,
until at last Leanne finished her incredible story.

She wasn't even sure if she thanked her friend for the vital
information, or if in fact she managed to say goodbye. She
only knew that when she had put the phone down and forced
herself to her feet, the silence was like a scream in her brain,
combining with the whirling thoughts that assailed her to
make her feel as if her skull was actually going to explode.

She took several unsteady steps towards Rafael, moving
like a sleepwalker with blank, unfocused eyes. She couldn't
even believe that this was the same man she had once known.
The man she had trusted, believed in, given her heart to. If
Leanne was right—and she could see no reason for her friend
to lie—then he had taken every bit of her trust and all the
love that was in her heart and used them callously for his
own ends.

'You…'

Her tongue felt thick and swollen, filling her mouth so that
she could get no words out.

Every trace of colour had leached from Rafael's face, leaving it ashen and drawn, his stunning eyes bleached and opaque. Even the raven's wing colour of his hair seemed dulled. And when he spoke his voice had the rusty, cracked sound of something that hasn't been used for so long it has totally seized up.

'She told you, didn't she?'

Serena could only nod numbly, still struggling to take in the enormity of what had happened to her. It couldn't be true. And yet Rafael's attitude seemed to imply...

'I'm sorry.'

The two simple words got through to her where nothing else had. Shattering the block of ice that seemed to have enclosed her ever since Leanne had started to speak, its bitter cold reaching right to her heart and freezing it to death, they freed her emotions from the shock that had held them numbed and dead.

'Is it true? Is what Leanne told me really what happened? Is it—?' Her voice cracked painfully. 'Rafael, is it *true*?'

At least he didn't try to pretend that he didn't know what she was talking about. That would have been the last, most bitter, the cruellest straw to break her back. As it was, she already felt as if the splintered shards of ice from the block that had enclosed her had all stabbed straight into her heart, lacerating it cruelly.

'*Es verdad*,' he said roughly. 'Yes, it's true.'

'No...'

It was a moan of distress, the sound of a wounded animal. Serena swayed on her feet, putting out a hand to the wall to support herself. She saw Rafael make a small, automatic move towards her to help, then, catching himself up, freeze again, and was deeply grateful. If he was to touch her then she knew that what little control she had left would be completely destroyed. She would shatter into a million pieces and she doubted if she could ever be made whole again.

'She said... She said...'

It seemed too impossible to put into words, but she had to try.

'She said that Tonio—is *mine*.'

Rafael's sombre eyes held hers, not flinching, not looking away once, not even blinking. She saw his answer in them before he even drew breath to speak.

'He is,' he said quietly. 'He's only my nephew, but he's your son—yours and Felipe's.'

'Mine...'

But it was too much for her poor, beleaguered brain to take in. With a choking cry, her hands fluttered up to her head, to press against her temples, pressing hard as if the small physical pain she inflicted on herself could counterbalance the searing anguish in her mind.

The buzzing inside her skull was getting worse. She couldn't feel her legs; they seemed to have turned to cotton wool, unable to support her. With what was left of her unfocused vision she saw Rafael's frown, vaguely heard him say something that might have been her name. But even as he moved forward, quickly this time, no hesitation, she loosened her precarious grip on consciousness and the darkness rolled up and over her, enclosing her completely.

When she came to herself again, she was lying on the huge gold settee in the sitting room, soft cushions at her head and feet. Opening her eyes slowly, she struggled to focus her fuzzy gaze on the man sitting opposite her, every muscle tense, hands clenched in his lap, his shadowed eyes fixed on her face.

'How do you feel?'

She hardly recognised it as Rafael's voice, it was so low and husky, almost hesitant.

'I—I don't know...'

Lifting her head carefully, she stared around at the room that suddenly seemed so strangely, subtly different. She couldn't quite work out what it was that was unfamiliar about it.

'Would you like a glass of water—coffee? Or something stronger?'

'Nothing…'

That was when it hit her. Her surroundings weren't *unfamiliar*; quite the opposite.

'The room! Rafael, I—I recognise it. Not from being here with you, but from before—with…'

'With Felipe?' With intuitive awareness he guessed exactly what she was trying to say, coming out of his chair and across the room to take her hands in his as he sat beside her on the settee. 'Serena, *querida*, is there anything else?'

'I don't know…'

Nervously she tested her thoughts, like someone pressing gently on a newly healed wound, checking to see if it was mending.

'I remember being here with Tonio and Felipe, and getting in the car…' Panic struck suddenly as a new memory formed in her head. 'Tonio was in the car too!'

'Yes, yes, he was. But he wasn't hurt,' Rafael hastened to assure her, seeing the concern in her eyes. 'He was in his carrycot, strapped in in the back, and he was completely unharmed. It was the driver's seat that took the worst of the impact. But what about before that? Can you remember anything earlier? Where did you meet Felipe?'

'At Leanne's wedding.'

The words came slowly as she struggled to pull coherent memories out of the whirling confusion of thoughts that piled one on top of the other in their haste to be recalled. After weeks and weeks of remembering nothing, now she was remembering *everything*, and it was a struggle to put them all into any coherent order.

'He was a friend of Mark's—Leanne's husband. They were at university together but Felipe was only there for a year.'

Rafael's beautiful mouth twisted wryly as he nodded his dark head.

'He got thrown out after failing his exams—and the re-sits. Studying was never Felipe's favourite thing. But he liked the student way of life and so he persuaded our father to give him an allowance while he found a new course that might suit him better. And when he failed at that he decided he wanted to be an artist, and then, I believe, a journalist—I'm afraid sticking power was not one of his major characteristics.'

'Oh!'

The little cry of distress wouldn't be held back. Immediately Rafael's bright eyes darkened and, realising that he still held her hands in his, he released them abruptly.

'I'm sorry. I forgot—you cared for him.'

Something in his voice jarred on her sensitised nerves. Pulling herself up on the cushions, she turned a frowning face towards him.

'And just what is that supposed to mean? You sound as if you doubt the truth of that statement.'

His breath hissed in sharply between his teeth as he raked both hands roughly through his black hair, ruining its sleek style.

'I don't know what you felt—what you thought of my brother. And to tell the truth I don't really care. But I know what he said about you... '

'Which was what?'

Suddenly restless, Rafael got to his feet and swung away from her, pacing across the room with the uneasy, restive movement of a caged tiger.

Disturbed by his reaction, and concerned to know what it meant, Serena stood up too and marched over to him, catching hold of his arm and bringing him to an abrupt halt.

'I said—which was what?'

Nothing good at all, to judge by Rafael's expression, the wary, tense look in his golden eyes.

'You'd better tell me,' she pressed him. 'Because I'm not

going to give up until you do. Just what did Felipe say to you about me?'

Rafael's free hand beat a restless tattoo against his thigh, the unsettled movement revealing more about his inward state of mind than his expression, which was schooled into a display of calm indifference that twisted painfully in Serena's stomach.

'He said that you were a cheap little tart.' The words came harshly, flung into her face with something that in any other man she would have called defiance, but which in Rafael's case seemed strangely almost like regret. 'That you picked him up at the wedding when you were half out of your mind on champagne—you threw yourself at him and made it plain that you were only too willing to go to bed with him then and there.'

If her memory hadn't come back, then this story might have hurt her, Serena reflected inwardly. But because she had already recalled just what Felipe Cordoba had been like nothing in what Rafael had told her upset her at all.

What really stung, eating away at her heart with the burn of acid, was that Rafael believed it. He had swallowed his brother's story whole. It was there in the blaze of scorn in his eyes, the contemptuous curl of his lip.

'What else?'

Was that cold, hard little voice really her own? It sounded so stiff, so brittle, that she could almost believe the words would shatter into pieces on the carpet in front of her.

Rafael pulled himself free of her restraining grasp and returned to his restless pacing. At the far side of the room he paused by the large, marble fireplace, staring down at it for a moment before swinging round to face her again.

'He said that all you were was a one-night stand. That he regretted ever meeting you even before the next morning. He came back to London and thought he'd never see you again, but...'

'But I tracked him down.' Serena completed the sentence

for him when, suddenly uncharacteristically at a loss for words, Rafael let it trail off. 'I turned up on his doorstep and told him I was pregnant and he was the father? I demanded that he support me and—what?—threatened him with blackmail if he didn't? Is that what he said?'

'No,' Rafael stunned her by saying.

'No?'

She had been so sure that was the story Felipe would have put about. That he would have wanted to paint her in the worst light possible, to make himself look the innocent victim in all this.

'What he actually said was that you tracked him down and turned up here with a baby you said was his—a baby you offered to sell him for a million pounds.'

'He said I...'

Once more Serena's brain refused to work. Refused to accept that Rafael had actually said what he had. That he had accused her of something so appalling, so absolutely, hatefully evil that she had trouble even grasping the idea, never mind believing that anyone could actually do it.

'He said that I wanted to *sell* Tonio? To sell my own baby—the one that I carried inside me, next to my heart, for nine long months? He said...'

'He said that you'd found out how wealthy our father is—how wealthy *I* am. That you'd never wanted the baby in the first place and the only reason you hadn't had it aborted was because you'd already thought of this plan. That—'

'No!' It was a high, moaning wail of pain. 'No! No! No! That wasn't what happened! It was never like that! Never! Do you hear me?'

Feeling the hot tears spring to her eyes, and knowing she was incapable of holding them back, she flung her hands up before her face, desperate to conceal her weakness from his cold, accusing glare.

'It was never like that,' she repeated brokenly.

There was a long, taut silence. Then she heard Rafael draw

in a deep, ragged breath and let it out again on a prolonged, weary-sounding sigh.

'Then why don't you tell me what it was like? Serena...'

Surprisingly gentle hands peeled her concealing fingers away from her face and lifted her chin so that her tear-washed brown eyes were forced to meet the amber scrutiny of his searching gaze.

'Tell me what really happened.'

When he looked at her like that, touched her like that, she would tell him anything, Serena told herself. When his eyes were so deep and dark and so disturbingly gentle, she felt as if they could reach right into her soul and draw out all that was in there. All the hurt. All the anger. All the loneliness. All the terrible, bitter sense of betrayal.

Betrayal.

The single word broke the spell, shattering her dream of trust and hope, revealing it for the pathetic fantasy that it was.

She couldn't trust Rafael any more than she'd been able to trust that hateful, selfish younger brother of his. Rafael had lied to her too. He had known all along that Tonio was hers— her baby—and he had lied through his teeth about it.

She had been betrayed by both Cordoba brothers, but while Felipe's behaviour had simply broken her spirit, leaving her bruised mind too hurt to remember his cruelty, Rafael's treachery had broken her heart.

CHAPTER THIRTEEN

'WHAT really happened!'

Flinging her fiery head back, to free herself from those restraining fingers, Serena faced him boldly, yellow flames of defiance blazing in her eyes.

'So you want to know the truth, do you? Well, I warn you—you won't like it.'

'Try me,' Rafael said softly, almost taking all the fight out of her with the two quiet words.

Almost, but not quite. All she had to do to get back her anger, revive the glorious, fear-defying rush of furious adrenaline, was to think of what Felipe had been planning. What he had told her he was going to do, right here in this room on that last night—the night of the car crash.

'Yes, I met Felipe at Leanne's wedding—and, yes, I got out of my head on champagne—champagne your brother pressed on me, knowing only too well that I was unused to anything alcoholic—champagne that, I learned later, he'd laced liberally with vodka.'

Rafael's violent curse slashed through her tirade, bringing her up short, but when she looked in his direction, expecting him to say something more, he simply made an impatient gesture with one hand, silently urging her to continue.

'I can't deny we ended up in bed together that night, but it was my bed—and Felipe forced his way in there, knowing full well that I was incapable of stopping him. He forced himself on me too...'

Her eyes were black with pain at the memory, her mouth trembling so much that she could hardly speak. But she had to go on. Had to make sure that Rafael knew the whole story.

168

After that he could believe her or not, as he liked. She was past caring.

'I—I had never slept with anyone before. I was a complete innocent. I was so foolishly naïve that I didn't even realise I was pregnant until I was over three months along. When I found out I was terrified. I had no money, no home, no one to turn to. Then I saw Felipe's picture in a newspaper—at some reception. That was when I came to London—trying to find him.'

'But why? After the way he had treated you?'

Serena's smile was twisted, her laugh distinctly shaky, perilously close to breaking down.

'Daft, wasn't it? But I had this crazy idea that perhaps I'd got him all wrong. That maybe he'd not meant to be so cruel. That when he found out I was pregnant he might want to help. And I—I thought that I owed it to him.'

'*Madre de Dios!*' Rafael's voice was raw with the shock that was etched onto his handsome features. 'Owed him *what*?'

'A chance to get to know his baby. A chance to be a father. It took me months to find where he lived. Months that wore me out, brought me near to collapse, so that when my baby was born I couldn't even feed him myself because I didn't have enough milk. That's when I lived in Norway Street. I only discovered Felipe's address just before Tonio was born. When he said I wasn't to worry, that he'd take care of everything, I believed him—I *believed* him!'

'Instead of which, what he really planned was to take your baby for himself and discard you again.'

Serena's eyes opened wide with shock at Rafael's quiet insertion.

'How did you know?'

'Serena, I knew my brother. I loved him, but that doesn't make me blind to his faults. He was a shallow, selfish, greedy young man. One who envied the money other people had, but was too lazy to make any for himself. By the time you met him he'd gone through every allowance my father gave him and then some. He'd started drinking heavily; he ran wild, became addicted to gambling and lost a fortune. Papá may be soft, but he's not a fool. He'd told Felipe that there was no more money for him unless he proved himself more responsible.'

'Tonio.' It was just a thin, weak breath of sound, but Rafael caught it and nodded grimly.

'I suspect that Tonio was to be presented to my father as the grandchild he wanted so much. A grandchild that he would have supported financially no matter what he thought of the child's father—one that Felipe knew I would help with too.'

Some instinct told Serena just what had put that new bitterness into his voice, made his mouth curl in distaste.

'You said you were on your way to England already...'

Rafael's nod of agreement was curt, grimly sombre.

'Felipe had rung me. He said he had just found out about the baby, and that you were offering Tonio for sale. He said he needed a million to pay you off or you'd go somewhere else.'

'And you were supposed to provide the cash?'

'He knew I'd do anything if there was a child involved, especially after the way my own son had died. I was to provide the money...'

The twist to his mouth became more pronounced, more thoughtfully bitter.

'Though I doubt if *you'd* have seen any of it. In the end it wasn't relevant. I arrived in England to hear about the crash. Felipe was dead and you were in the hospital.'

The woman he had believed was little more than a tart, one who was selfish and grasping enough to be prepared to sell her own child to the highest bidder. So why had he bothered to take care of her?

What was it he had said in the hospital on the day that he had first brought Tonio to see her—a day that she now looked back on from such a very different perspective now that her eyes were newly opened?

I felt responsible. That was what he'd said, and, being Rafael, he had shouldered this unwanted legacy from his brother no matter what his personal distaste for the burden.

Slowly she turned away from him, needing a few moments of peace, to think without the distractions of his tall, strong frame, his devastatingly attractive features—and the fact that she had believed herself so deeply in love with him.

And what did she feel now? She couldn't answer that question. Deep in her heart, under the scars and the bruises, perhaps something of what she had felt still burned, but she didn't really know. And she hadn't got time to dig down and try to find it—wasn't even sure that she wanted to. Because there was so much more that she still needed to sort out in her own mind.

'So you took on the responsibility for me and for my baby,' she said, staring fixedly out of the window into the darkness beyond. She could see Rafael's lean frame reflected in front of her and so saw him make a movement towards her, then still, as he had done when she had been on the phone. 'But you didn't tell me Tonio was mine.'

'Serena, you know why that was. You were weak, hurt, and you couldn't remember. The doctors advised—'

'Oh, I know what the doctors advised!' Serena cut in bitterly. 'But be honest, Rafael. That advice suited you down to the ground, didn't it?'

When he didn't answer, his only response being to become even stiller, his eyes just deep, dark pools in his reflected face, she turned slowly, unwillingly, forcing herself to confront him again. She knew that the pain of her suspicions had drained all the colour from her own cheeks and she saw his quick, uneasy frown as he met her shadowed gaze.

'Tell me about your own child, Rafael. The baby who died with Elena. Because that was what happened to it, wasn't it?'

'Yes.'

It was a long, deep sigh of sadness and resignation as his amber gaze dropped to the floor, affecting an intense interest in the pattern of the carpet.

'Yes, he died when she did. When Elena discovered she had cancer, she refused all treatment, hoping that at least our baby would live. But she was sicker than we had ever thought. She died before she was sixth months pregnant, and our son died in her womb.'

'And how long ago was this?'

'Eighteen months.'

Suddenly his head came up again, and the mixture of pain and futile anger in his face was terrible to see, making Serena flinch inside in anguished sympathy.

'I would have done anything to save him. I would have given my life if it had meant he would have lived.'

She didn't doubt it for a second. It was what she had expected.

'And so you wanted my child.'

'*Dios!* No!'

'The truth, Rafael! Are you saying you didn't want Tonio?'

Looking into his face, she saw the moment it changed. Saw the darkness take over his eyes, the uncomfortable set of his jaw. And in that moment something very beautiful but very, very vulnerable died inside her, shrivelling into ashes in her heart.

'I came to London to sort out an appalling mess that you and Felipe seemed to have created between you.'

Rafael spoke slowly, reluctantly, the words seeming to have to be dragged from the bottom of his soul.

'I'd been sold the story that you were a mercenary, grasping witch, who would hand her baby over to anyone for the right price. And I sure as hell knew that unless my brother got his act together fast he was no fit person to be a father to anyone. I thought I could pay you off, take the baby, and hand him over to his grandparents—my mother and father—who would love to take care of him.'

In a gesture of intense weariness he rubbed the back of his hand across his wide forehead, as if hoping to erase the backlog of memories that lingered in his thoughts.

'But I hadn't reckoned on two things. The first was that I took one look at Tonio and fell head over heels in love. I wanted to take on the world for him, protect him, love him, be a father to him. And I needed him. I'd lost my own son, and now it seemed like I was getting a second chance.'

'And so you kept my son from me.'

Was this how it felt when your heart broke? Serena wondered sadly. Was it really not with the raw, tearing pain that she had feared, but instead with this dull, aching sense of—of nothing? It was as if every nerve, every sense was numbed, unable to feel, so that there was just a great empty space deep inside her.

'You didn't tell me about him because you wanted him for your own.'

'No!' Rafael declared furiously, amber eyes blazing in angry denial. 'It wasn't like that at all. At the beginning—before you came round—I had no idea you'd suffer from amnesia, so I stuck to my original plan to buy you off. Then I realised that you couldn't remember a thing, not even about Tonio, and I had to rethink, fast.'

He had resumed his uneasy pacing up and down the room as he spoke, the long, restless panther strides betraying more about his unsettled state of mind than his obvious ruthless determination to give her the facts as calmly and coherently as possible.

'The doctors were insistent that you should be left to remember things in your own time. That no one should force the pace or push you into anything you didn't want to think about. They said it was far more likely that your inability to remember was in fact more like a refusal to do so. That your amnesia was protecting you from some trauma that you didn't have the strength to face.'

'So when you brought Tonio to me in the hospital, it was—what? Some sort of a test?'

On the far side of the room Rafael stilled, looking her straight in the face, meeting her eyes without any hesitation.

'Dr Greene said it was worth a try. And I had to see how you were with the baby. Amnesia is like hypnotism. Just as you can't be forced to do something you believe is morally wrong, even in a trance, you can never forget your real, true self. The moment I saw how you reacted to Tonio, even when you thought he was mine, I knew that Felipe hadn't been telling me the whole truth. That was when I decided to bring you here.'

'To keep me a prisoner—under surveillance—while you decided whether I was fit to look after my son or not?'

'It wasn't like that, Serena. I swear it wasn't. I wanted to give you the material comfort and security you'd been seeking when—if you'd asked Felipe for money. And I wanted to give you some time to be with your son and hopefully to bond with him so that when you got your memory back you could be a true mother to him.'

'But...'

Serena shook her head in confusion at the way he seemed to have contradicted the things he had said earlier.

'But you've already admitted that you needed Tonio. That your parents needed their grandson. Why would you—?'

'Because *Tonio* needed *you*! You're his mother, for God's sake! And, having seen the way you reacted to him, I was sure that you needed him too, even if you didn't yet know it.'

'And—and if I'd failed all these tests you set me? If in the end you'd decided I wasn't a fit sort of mother for Tonio?'

For the great Rafael Cordoba's nephew, a bitter little voice inside her head added, twisting her nerve-ends into cruel knots.

'What if I really had been after the money?'

'Then you'd have received a bigger pay-off than your covetous little mind could ever have imagined and been sent on your way—but only after you'd signed some completely watertight documents making me Tonio's legal guardian for the rest of my life.'

So now she knew exactly why he had made the promise that he wouldn't let her hurt anyone on the day he had brought her here from the hospital. He had had everything planned down to the last detail, like a master chess player, and she had just been a very small pawn on the board he was using.

'Do you know what I really don't understand?' she flung at him, an agony of bitterness wrenching the words from her mouth even though a strong sense of self-preservation warned her to hold them back. 'I don't see why you didn't just take Tonio and go. After all, that was what your damn brother was going to do, so why should you be any different? Why did you ever bother with me?'

'Why...?'

Rafael crossed the space between them in several long, determined strides. Coming to a halt barely feet away from her, he looked down into her unhappy face, golden eyes searching every inch of it with a searing intensity that made her flinch as if his gaze could actually burn her.

And then, amazingly, he smiled. A gentle smile, but one that was touched with sadness, and no light from it touched his eyes, leaving them clouded and sombre as before.

'Don't you know, Serena? Haven't you guessed? I said that when I came to England I hadn't reckoned on two things. I've told you the first. The second shocked me even more. The truth is, *querida*, that I took one look at you and wanted you more than I've ever wanted any woman in my life. It was like being struck by a lightning bolt. I couldn't think—

I couldn't even breathe! I could no sooner have taken Tonio and left you behind than I could have stopped my heart beating.'

And, oh, she knew how that felt, didn't she? Hadn't she been through the same experience when she had first opened her eyes and looked into Rafael's stunning face? Hadn't she really known then, deep down, that this man was her fate, her once in a lifetime destiny, and that if she didn't grasp the opportunity with both hands then her existence would always be the poorer for it?

'And—and now?'

'Now?'

Stunning her completely, he took her hand in his, then sank to one knee on the carpet before her, looking up into her bemused face with dark, serious eyes.

'Now I know I can never let you go. It would kill me if I did. I want you to marry me...'

This couldn't be happening! Serena could only shake her head in disbelief. Was it possible that Rafael, arrogant, confident, forceful Rafael Cordoba, the Spanish Inquisitor himself, was actually on his knees before her, asking...?

'No?' Rafael had seen her shake her head and misinterpreted her reasons for it. 'Your answer is no?'

'I don't know what my answer is! I can't think...'

With a groan of self-reproach, Rafael pushed his free hand through the black silk of his hair, ruffling it wildly so that Serena longed to be able to reach out and smooth it back into place. She didn't dare to put the wish into practice, though. Simply by touching him she might ignite that incendiary passion that flared between them so easily and destroyed all chance of thought.

And she had to think. Her future and the future of her baby depended on it.

'You—you told me that you didn't love me...'

'*Madre de Dios!*' Rafael muttered thickly. 'When I said that I was angry, confused. I had believed that you were not as my brother had told me, but that day we went to Norway Street suddenly you changed. You made it plain that you appreciated the wealth I had, the things I'd bought—and that you were prepared to offer sexual favours in return.'

'I was scared, shocked by the reality of Norway Street! And *you* seemed so different. I was afraid that when you saw where I'd come from you'd turn away from me.'

'I would never have done that. But I didn't know which was the real Serena. The woman I was only just beginning to realise I cared for so much, or this new, seductive siren, who fitted much more with my brother's story.'

The strong fingers that held hers tightened convulsively, communicating his remembered feelings.

'And then, completely out of the blue, you announce that you love me. I didn't know whether you meant it or if it was just a clever way of making sure that you kept me firmly clamped to your side to provide for you.'

'No!'

It was Serena's turn to tighten her grip, twisting her fingers in his until they were holding instead of being held.

'Such a thought never even crossed my mind. I love you too much.'

'Then you'll marry me? You'll be my wife and you and Tonio will come and live with me...'

You and Tonio. Serena found that her small white teeth were digging into the softness of her lower lip with such ferocity that she was surprised they hadn't drawn blood.

You and *Tonio.* If he had left those words unspoken then she might have given him his answer.

She would have said yes and might now be in his arms, being held close, feeling his kisses, being Rafael Cordoba's *fiancée.* She would even have been happy about it. Because right at this moment she felt that she had never loved him half as much as she did now.

But he had said those fateful words, and by doing so had turned the whole situation upside down. He'd said them and so now she couldn't give the answer she had wanted to give, but had instead to say... 'No.'

'No?'

It was the last thing he had expected, that much was clear. Shock leached the colour from his face, brought him to his feet in a rush, made him release her fingers to fasten his hands instead around her upper arms, actually giving her the tiniest shake before he collected himself again.

'Why no? Serena, you can't mean this. You can't do this to me—to us. I know that you love me. I've told you how much I love you...'

'It isn't enough.'

She would never know how she forced the words out. Every syllable seemed to stick in her throat, scraping over tender tissues so that her voice was raw and husky, quavering weakly and threatening to desert her completely.

'Not enough? Serena, *cariña*, I'll give you anything you want—everything you want. I'll give you the world...'

'Rafael, don't!'

It was a high-pitched cry of agony, flung at him in a desperate attempt to stop him. Burning tears were streaming down her face, blurring his features in front of her, but she could see his eyes, his fierce, golden eyes, and she fixed her own bruised gaze on them, pleading with him to understand.

'Don't make things worse. Don't make this harder for me than it already is. Please understand...'

'Understand?'

She could hear his retreat in his voice. He was the old Rafael again, cold and hard and agonisingly distant.

'I swear to God I do not understand a word you are saying, or the reasons behind them. I have told you I love you, that I want to marry you...'

'But do you want *me*? Do you want me for myself or because I come as a package with Tonio? Would you want to marry me no matter what? Or am I just someone you care enough about to tolerate because of the child you want so much—the child I can provide?'

She had never experienced a silence so oppressive, so terrible as the one that followed her outburst. In that silence she could almost see the wall of ice forming around Rafael, cutting him off from her, and although he was still standing directly in front of her, still had his hands on her arms, she felt as if he was physically backing away from her, putting as much distance between them as possible.

'If I were to answer that,' he said at last, just in time to stop the tension getting to her so much that she actually screamed from the pain of it, 'then you would not believe my love even if I declared it over and over, a hundred thousand times. You think I only want you for Tonio, and any attempt to convince you otherwise will only go to show just *how much* I want him, and so condemn me in your eyes. And if I say, yes, that is the case, I only want the mother to get the son, then you will reject my proposal out of hand. It seems to me that this is a no-win situation.'

Belatedly becoming aware of the way he still held her, he lifted his hands away, opening them wide as if to demonstrate that he was setting her free.

'And, that being the case, I will do as you ask. I will make this as easy as possible for you. So—come...'

Serena stared in bemusement at the hand he held out to her, the so-familiar autocratic gesture transmuted into a disturbingly gentle appeal.

Because of that she could do nothing but what he asked, putting her hand into his once more and allowing him to draw her to his side, following blindly as he led her from the room.

He took her up the long, curving flight of stairs and down the landing, past her bedroom, and his, where so many nights they had lain together and made blazing, passionate love. She had guessed just where he was taking her and so it was no surprise when he opened the door to Tonio's room—*her baby's* room—and drew her inside.

At the side of the cot he released her, stepping forward and bending over the sleeping child. With infinite gentleness he lifted the baby from the mattress, each movement so slow and careful that Tonio never even stirred.

For several long, silent moments Rafael simply looked down into the face of the baby, the expression on his face reminding Serena of the moment she had come looking for Tonio and found Rafael sitting cross-legged on the bed, holding him. One long, tanned finger stroked the top of the small head, traced the curving line of his cheek, and then, drawing in his breath sharply, Rafael bent and kissed the baby's delicate forehead.

'*Adiós, mi corazón,*' he whispered, then, turning to Serena, he held the baby out to her. 'Take him, Serena. Here is your son.'

Her son. Serena folded her arms around the sturdy, breathing warmth of the baby and held him close, feeling as if her head would actually burst under the pressure of all the feelings that were in it. She cradled Tonio against her breast, breathed in the warm, sweet baby smell of him, rubbed her nose against his hair and wept for the days, the weeks when she hadn't known he was hers.

'Thank God I have you back,' she whispered in his sleeping ear. 'Thank God!'

She didn't know how long it was that she stood there, lost in her love for this child of hers. Didn't know whether a minute or an hour had passed before some faint noise downstairs caught her attention and dragged her back to the present. She only knew that when she looked around she was alone. Rafael had gone, and she hadn't even heard him leave.

Rafael!

Suddenly it came to her what she had heard. The sound of the front door opening. The noise of the car boot being opened and then shut again.

Rafael.

Gently, so as not to disturb him, she laid Tonio back in

his cot. She would have his lifetime to give her son all the love that was in her heart. Some powerful inner instinct told her that if she didn't hurry she would lose the chance to do the same for the other beloved male in her life.

She was only just in time. Rafael was just coming back into the hall to collect the suitcase that stood at the bottom of the stairs. Beyond the open front door, his car stood ready. She could even see his keys in the ignition.

'Rafael, wait!'

Her call stopped him dead, looking up at her in shock.

Serena's heart clenched painfully at the sight of him, the shadows under his eyes, the lines around his nose and mouth. He seemed to have aged ten years in the short time since she had seen him.

'What are you doing? Where are you going?'

'I'm leaving. Going back to Spain.' It was succinct to the point of curtness.

'But why?'

'Serena, you know why! You won't believe I love you, except as Tonio's mother, and I can't stay here—can't endure being with you and not being able to love you! So it's better that I leave. I've left a letter here...'

A wave of his hand indicated a long white envelope lying on the oak hall table.

'Take it to my solicitor—the address is on it—and he'll sort everything out for you. Obviously Tonio will be entitled to everything that should have been his father's, but I've also made sure you'll be comfortable in your own right. I'm giving you the house...'

'Giving me the house!' Shock gave Serena the impetus to move, running swiftly down the stairs to come to his side. 'But, Rafael, why?'

'Because I want you to have everything you need. I want you to be secure, to be free to live your life in whatever way makes you happy. '

Turning to her, he lifted his free hand and touched it to

her cheek, cupping the curve of her face gently in its warmth as the pad of his thumb traced the softness of her mouth.

'Be happy, Serena,' he urged softly. 'Promise me that.'

For one long second more his dark amber eyes lingered on her mouth, as if he longed to press his lips onto its fullness. But then he shook his head sharply, almost snatched his hand away and turned to the door. Serena drew in a sharply jagged breath. It was now or never.

'Rafael!' she called after him, louder than was actually necessary because she feared that at this vital moment her voice might desert her. 'Don't go!'

He stilled, but he didn't swing round. His proud head remained turned towards the door, his suitcase in his hand.

'What did you say?' His voice was rough and thick, sounding rusty from not being used.

'I said don't go! Don't leave me, please!'

That brought him to face her at last, his movements looking strangely like a film played in slow motion.

'I can't stay, Serena. I can't live here with you and not be able to have you as my wife. It would break my heart.'

And if she had had even the slightest trace of doubt left in her mind then that emotional avowal would have erased it for good.

'Then do that,' she told him softly. 'Stay with me and marry me and be a father to Tonio.'

The sound of the suitcase hitting the floor as his grasp on it loosened made her heart leap in joy. But still Rafael didn't move. Still he didn't come to her.

'Why?' was all he said.

'There's a saying,' Serena said carefully, wanting, needing to get this exactly right. 'Something about if you want something very badly, then let it go free. If it goes, it was never yours in the first place, but if it comes back to you then it's yours for ever.'

She had his full attention now. He was watching, waiting, his eyes burning into her.

'That's what you did for me, Rafael. You let me go free—
gave me the greatest gift any man could give me. You gave
me my son, and my life, and if I'd wanted it you were prepared to walk out and leave me to enjoy it—you—'

Her voice splintered, breaking in the middle.

'You were even prepared to give me the income I needed
and the house... But I don't want the money, Rafael, I don't
want this house that wouldn't be a home without you. All I
want is you. If you'll have me, I want to come back to you,
my darling. I'm coming back and I want to stay for ever.'

She didn't see him move. Only felt his arms come round
her, his heart beating frantically in unison with hers. She felt
his mouth on her lips, warm and demanding, but most of all
so, so loving.

For a long, long time she was adrift on a heated sea of
sensation, lost to the world, to everything except this man
whom she loved more than life itself. But eventually reality
returned and she came slowly back down to earth, looking
deep into Rafael's darkened eyes and seeing there her own
love mirrored and returned a thousandfold.

'So you will marry me.' Rafael's voice was deep, husky
with the intensity of his feelings.

'I'll marry you,' she whispered, her smile growing as she
saw the light of pure joy in his face.

'I want nothing more than to be your husband, and I'll try
to be the best father to Tonio that I can.'

'You'll be all the father he'll ever need,' she assured him
with total confidence. 'He'll be your child of love—truly
your love-child—and that's what matters most. And perhaps
one day we'll have a brother or a sister for him to add to our
family. And as for me, I know you'll be so much more of a
husband than I could ever have dreamed of.'

Rafael's deep, wide smile made her heart sing, and another
of those fierce, demanding kisses set her heart thudding in
excitement, the blood heating in her veins.

'I promise you I'll fill your days with every happiness I

can think of, and your nights with all the passion that's in my heart for you,' he told her, gathering her close to him again.

It was a promise for life. And Serena knew that Rafael always kept his promises.

He's a man of cool sophistication.
He's got pride, power and wealth.
He's a ruthless businessman, an expert lover—
and he's one hundred percent committed
to staying single.

Until now. Because suddenly he's responsible
for a BABY!

HIS BABY

An exciting miniseries from Harlequin Presents®
He's sexy, he's successful...
and now he's facing up to fatherhood!

On sale February 2001:
RAFAEL'S LOVE-CHILD
by Kate Walker, Harlequin Presents® #2160

On sale May 2001:
MORGAN'S SECRET SON
by Sara Wood, Harlequin Presents® #2180

And look out for more later in the year!

Available wherever Harlequin books are sold.

HARLEQUIN®
Makes any time special ™

Visit us at www.eHarlequin.com

HPBABY

#1 *New York Times* bestselling author

NORA ROBERTS

brings you more of the loyal and loving,
tempestuous and tantalizing Stanislaski family.

Coming in February 2001

The Stanislaski Sisters

Natasha and Rachel

Though raised in the Old World traditions of their
family, fiery Natasha Stanislaski and cool, classy
Rachel Stanislaski are ready for a *new* world of love....

*And also available in February 2001 from
Silhouette Special Edition, the newest book in the
heartwarming Stanislaski saga*

CONSIDERING KATE

Natasha and Spencer Kimball's daughter Kate turns her
back on old dreams and returns to her hometown, where
she finds the *man* of her dreams.

Available at your favorite retail outlet.

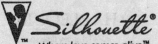

Where love comes alive™

**Lindsay Armstrong...
Helen Bianchin...
Emma Darcy...
Miranda Lee...**

Some of our bestselling writers are Australians!

Look our for their novels about the Wonder from Down Under—where spirited women win the hearts of Australia's most eligible men.

THE AUSTRALIANS

Coming soon:

THE MARRIAGE RISK
by Emma Darcy
On sale February 2001, Harlequin Presents® #2157

And look out for:

MARRIAGE AT A PRICE
by Miranda Lee
On sale June 2001, Harlequin Presents® #2181

Available wherever Harlequin books are sold.

HARLEQUIN®
Makes any time special ™

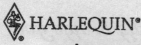